10 47

MAKE-BELIEVE
MARRIAGE

MAKE-BELIEVE MARRIAGE

•

Marilyn Shank

AVALON BOOKS
NEW YORK

c. 1

PRINTED IN THE UNITED STATES OF AMERICA
ON ACID-FREE PAPER
BY HADDON CRAFTSMEN, BLOOMSBURG, PENNSYLVANIA

Dedicated with love to the educators in our family:
my brother Ralph, my husband John,
and our daughters Debbie and Mindi.

Chapter One

Claire Jennings hurried down the shaded paths of the school campus, barely noticing the songbirds or the heavy scent of marigolds lingering on the late-summer breeze. She couldn't be a minute late for her 10:00 appointment. This interview was her chance.

She pulled open the heavy wooden door of Mason Hall, took a seat in the reception area, and propped her briefcase against the leg of her chair. Because the upcoming interview had left her too excited to eat breakfast, she'd taken her sinus medication on an empty stomach and she felt a little shaky.

The receptionist called her name, then led Claire down a narrow hallway. They stopped in front of an open door where an inordinately handsome man in a navy pinstripe suit sat behind a large oak desk. "Mr. Mathison, Claire Jennings to see you," the receptionist announced.

1

When the man stood and strode toward her, Claire sensed an irresistible magnetism about him. She hoped she could concentrate in the presence of this tall, great-looking administrator. He extended his hand. "Welcome, Miss Jennings. I'm Trevor Mathison, Headmaster of Brookshire School for Young Ladies."

Claire slipped her hand into his. His fingers wrapped around hers and his warm touch made her heart skip a beat. "Happy to meet you, Mr. Mathison."

"Please take a seat."

She perched on the edge of the chair and the headmaster returned to his desk. "I understand you're applying for our sixth grade position. Do you have any teaching experience, Miss Jennings?"

"Not yet. I just graduated from Rockhurst College last week."

"Then perhaps you'd show me a copy of your résumé."

Claire reached for the briefcase she'd propped against the leg of her chair, suddenly remembering it was the waiting room chair she'd propped it up against. She took a steadying breath. "I'm afraid I left my briefcase in the foyer. I'll go and get it."

The man's brow creased slightly and he reached for his telephone. "Never mind. Diane will bring it."

Great. She couldn't even remember to bring her briefcase to the interview. At least she'd gotten it into the building. Claire smiled pleasantly, as if expecting the receptionist to deliver your briefcase was common practice.

Several minutes dragged painfully past and the handsome man studied her through the whole embarrassing ordeal. Finally, the young woman returned with the briefcase. "Thanks so much," Claire said politely.

She hurriedly shuffled through several sheets of paper and handed one to the headmaster. "Here you are, sir."

He scanned the information, then glanced up at her. "Since you have no teaching experience, what in your background qualifies you to be a Brookshire teacher?"

"I spent a year in Europe," she said, hoping to impress this commanding person.

"Employed or as a student?"

"Employed."

If only he'd leave it at that. But the questioning look in his fascinating eyes made Claire finish the story. "I studied plants and herbs in Europe and supported myself as a waitress."

His interest waned. "I see."

As he continued reviewing the résumé, Claire tried to ignore the butterflies that had congregated in her stomach and were having it out with the sinus medication.

Laying the résumé aside, the headmaster looked squarely at her. His eyes were the darkest brown she'd ever seen. Could they be black? Did anyone have black eyes?

"Where did you do your student teaching, Miss Jennings?"

"At Briarfield Elementary in the Kansas City District."

The headmaster's penetrating gaze never left her face. "Perhaps you could explain your disciplinary approach."

Her disciplinary approach? She fervently wished she'd eaten breakfast, because now the sinus medication was making her a little lightheaded as well. "I think children should discipline themselves. Whenever possible."

He raised eyebrows as ominously dark as his eyes. "Would you care to elaborate?"

"I believe self-discipline is the most effective kind."

Now he looked frustrated. "No one would argue with that premise, Miss Jennings. But in a school of three hundred young girls, self-discipline does not run rampant. But students *will,* given the opportunity. In my view, a Brookshire teacher has two primary functions: to set a sterling example and to be a strict disciplinarian. Otherwise chaos reigns."

The man was another Jacob Lawrence, Claire decided. Had her grandfather been reincarnated as the extremely handsome Headmaster of Brookshire School? That wasn't possible. Grandfather Lawrence was alive and well. And just as strong-minded as Trevor Mathison.

The interview wasn't going well. Claire toyed with telling the headmaster her grandfather was Chairman of the Board of Brookshire School but decided against it. She'd land this job on her own merits or not at all.

Mr. Mathison glanced at his watch and Claire knew he wished their session was over. If she didn't start agreeing with the man, she'd never get hired.

She swallowed hard, ready to try anything. "I wholeheartedly agree with your definition of a good teacher, Mr. Mathison. A teacher should set a good example and discipline students as needed."

He seemed somewhat mollified. "Let me ask you another question. What do you consider your strong points? As a teacher, I mean?"

Strong points, strong points. "Well, I'm creative," she replied. "I believe that creativity facilitates learning. Too many teachers get locked into traditional teaching methods that bore their students.

"And I'm also flexible and broad-minded," Claire continued. "I want to provide my students with diverse learning experiences."

He didn't seem the slightest bit impressed and was checking his watch again. "Thank you for coming in, Miss Jennings. I have several people left to interview, but if you are selected for the position, I'll get word to you in a day or so."

When he got to his feet, Claire's heart sank. The headmaster had just dismissed her. He expected her to get up and leave his office. But she couldn't. This job was her last hope.

"Mr. Mathison, I know this interview didn't go well. May I say something in my own defense?"

He looked wary but sat back down. "What is it, Miss Jennings?"

"If I seem disorganized it's because I was too nervous to eat breakfast and I took some sinus medication on an empty stomach. But I want to assure you that I will be a first-rate teacher. I have good rapport with children. We connect. If you hire me, Mr. Mathison, you won't regret it. You have my word on that."

Trevor rubbed his forehead and sighed. Why, when he was frantically busy and desperate to find a qualified teacher, luck had sent him Claire Jennings? Bad luck, that is! The only positive thing he could say about this woman was that she was gorgeous. Hair as blond as liquid sunshine and eyes the color of a midsummer sky. With her abundant good looks, she could be a model.

She *should* be a model, because Miss Jennings would never be a teacher. At least not at Brookshire School.

He cleared his throat. "Barbara Danson, the teacher I'm replacing, was a strict disciplinarian. She employed traditional teaching methods, which work well for us here. My goal is to hire a teacher very like Mrs. Danson. One who uses strict discipline and can keep the sixth-grade class under excellent control."

The woman said nothing but stared at him with those incredible eyes. The clearest blue eyes he'd ever seen. For a moment, he forgot what he was talking about.

He quickly pulled himself together. "Look, I'm sorry, Miss Jennings, but I can't offer you the job. The girls coming into sixth grade are a difficult group and I will probably hire an experienced teacher for this position. I'm being frank with you so you can continue your job search and secure a position before the fall term begins."

She leaned forward and Trevor saw anxiety spark in those lovely eyes. "But there are no other openings. School starts next week and all the area districts have their positions filled."

He softened a bit as those amazing eyes probed his very soul. "I wish I could help you, but . . ."

"This was my last chance to . . ." She stopped mid-sentence.

"To teach? Surely not."

Suddenly, Claire Jennings's cornflower blue eyes brimmed with tears. Trevor couldn't bear to see a woman cry. Why hadn't he ushered her out sooner?

She sniffed delicately. "You don't understand. It's Granddad's ultimatum."

That sinus medication had jumbled her thoughts bigtime. Trevor knew he should leave well enough alone, but he found himself suddenly curious. "An ultimatum? I'm afraid I don't understand."

She sighed and her obvious concern tugged at his heart. "My grandfather hasn't approved of my choices in life, and on my birthday five years ago he gave me an ultimatum. According to that ultimatum, I'm supposed to be happily married with a successful career just four weeks from today. Otherwise, my inheritance goes to charity."

"You mean you give your grandfather that kind of power over you? Just to get his money?"

The lovely lady's expression turned indignant. "I don't care a whit about Granddad's money. But I do care about *him.* I love him in spite of his eccentricities." She bit her lip, then continued. "You see, Granddad equates love with money. When he withholds his money, he's showing his disappoval. He's taking his love."

She shook her head and her shiny hair bobbed around her slim shoulders. "How can I expect you to understand something I don't understand myself?"

Ridiculous as it seemed, Trevor did understand. He'd been presented with a similar ultimatum by the Brookshire Board of Directors. They almost hadn't hired him last year because of his bachelor status. And at Trevor's recent evaluation, the board made it painfully clear that for longevity at Brookshire, he needed a wife. Ironically, he and the lovely Claire Jennings had the same problem.

If she wanted to keep her grandfather's love, and if he wanted to keep his headmaster position, marriage was essential.

But Trevor couldn't tell Miss Jennings that. And he couldn't hire her, either. The woman simply wasn't Brookshire material. She reminded him of Jessica Mason, his former fiancée. Jessica was a free spirit and Trevor had learned the hard way that you couldn't trust that type of woman.

He shrugged. "I sympathize with your problem, but I'm afraid that won't affect my decision."

She stood and squared her pretty shoulders. "Then there's nothing more to say."

When they shook hands, Trevor noticed how soft her hand felt in his. For a moment he wished Claire Jennings was a different personality. Tougher. Stronger. Someone who could take on a classroom of thirty sixth-graders and survive the experience.

"Good luck with your teaching career," he said.

Her lovely lips formed a smile but it didn't reach her eyes. "Thanks for your time, Mr. Mathison."

When Miss Jennings left, Diane ushered in his next appointment, a Mrs. Caroline Mulligan. And while she had excellent credentials, the middle-aged woman had no spark at all to distract Trevor from the interview. She seemed pretty lackluster and boring after Claire Jennings.

Late that afternoon, Trevor shuffled through the stack of résumés he'd acquired during the week-long interviewing process. He'd hoped to hire a teacher today, but now it would have to wait until after the weekend. With classes starting Wednesday, making the selection was critical.

As he reviewed the applicants, his thoughts strayed to Claire Jennings. Her remembered how her long blond hair curved softly at her shoulders, how her blue eyes sparked with enthusiasm. And how her long legs went on *ad infinitum.* Was it only Miss Jennings's great looks that kept bringing her into his thoughts?

No. It was that ridiculous ultimatum her grandfather had issued. It smacked of coercion. But Trevor could sympathize with the man in one respect. He wanted to help shape his granddaughter's out-of-control life. Make her more responsible. It seemed Miss Jennings couldn't achieve that on her own.

It had been tough to tell the lovely lady she wasn't Brookshire material, but he'd had no choice. That was his job. She'd looked so disappointed, he felt a little like Ebenezer Scrooge kicking Tiny Tim.

As Trevor put away the file folders he'd been reviewing, he noticed a briefcase propped against the leg of a chair. He sighed. It could only belong to one person. Claire Jennings.

This was another example of the woman's lack of discipline. He'd telephone her and have her pick it up.

He fished her résumé from the stack and perused it again.

Personal Experience: *Spent two years in the Far East studying Tai Chi and Transcendental Meditation. Lived in Europe for a year studying plants and herbs.* Job Experience: *Manager of a health food store; waitress.*

Trevor shook his head. She was one zany lady.

He checked the résumé for her address and phone number. At least it proved helpful for that. She lived at 509 Mulberry Lane, in Fairfield, Missouri. He also lived in Fairfield, a small Kansas City suburb just twenty miles south of Brookshire School. It would be simpler to deliver her briefcase and be done with it.

As Trevor drove toward Fairfield, he glanced at his gas gauge, surprised that it registered almost empty. He usually filled the tank when the needle reached a quarter full. But he'd been swamped with job interviews and hadn't taken the time. He would stop for gas after he returned the briefcase.

As he turned onto Mulberry Lane, he admired the neat, picturesque neighborhood. The homes were well tended and the lawns immaculately manicured. Late-summer flowers bloomed in orderly profusion and children Rollerbladed down the sidewalks.

Trevor located the address and knocked on the front door of a white cottage with blue-shuttered windows and lavish red geraniums spilling from the flower boxes.

No answer. He should have phoned first.

As he started to leave, Claire Jennings opened the door. Her pretty face lit with pleasure. "Mr. Mathison! You came to offer me the job!"

He should have seen this coming. Now he had to disappoint the pretty lady all over again. "I didn't come to hire you, Miss Jennings—just to return your briefcase."

For the second time that day, the disappointment on her face tugged at his heart.

"I see," she said, enthusiasm draining from her voice. "I shouldn't jump to conclusions." She shrugged. "No hard feelings, though. Won't you come in for a cup of tea?"

He didn't want to, but he hated rejecting her again— hated to see any more disappointment in those enticing blue eyes. "Just one cup," he mumbled grudgingly, following her inside.

"Have a seat on the couch and I'll pour your tea."

Trevor watched her blow out a candle that rested in an ornate golden candlestick in the middle of her living room floor. "Are you expecting a power failure?" he asked.

When she smiled, Trevor noticed that her skin was as flawless as porcelain, and her lips full and inviting.

"I was meditating. Focusing on a candle flame helps me center my thoughts."

Fruitcake city, Trevor thought to himself. He'd drink her tea, then head for the Hereford House Restaurant. It had been a particularly stressful week and a thick, juicy steak would help him unwind. "Do you really believe in that meditation stuff?"

"Absolutely. Meditation helps me get my head on straight."

Meditation had a ways to go where Miss Jennings was concerned.

She walked to a tea cart and poured from a china pot. "You've had a hectic day, Mr. Mathison. This will help you relax."

Should he drink it? She wouldn't poison him, would she? Just because he hadn't hired her?

A sudden pain shot up Trevor's shoulder into his neck. He rotated his neck stiffly, realizing he had accumulated a lot of tension.

"Your neck is stiff," she said sympathetically.

"A little."

"I do Swedish massage. In five minutes, I can have you so relaxed you'll hardly be able to walk out of here."

Candles, meditation, and Swedish massage! He should do more than walk out of here. He should flee for his sanity.

Before he could extricate himself, Claire Jennings slipped behind the couch and began massaging his neck. Her soft touch startled him and he started to protest. But before he managed to, her hands began working their magic. Within moments, the tension that had been building all week began to dissipate.

Claire knew it was presumptuous to massage the headmaster's neck. But she'd had two premonitions this afternoon that Trevor Mathison would, indeed, hire her to teach at Brookshire School.

One premonition came while she meditated. When she'd started, she was tied in emotional knots from the stress of rejection. But as she continued, a deep sense of peace enveloped her and she felt a strong assurance that she would get this job.

She read the second confirmation in the tea leaves. But since Mr. Mathison hadn't received any such insight, she'd have to keep him here until she could convince him that she was his woman.

Well, not *his* woman. But certainly the woman for the job.

When Claire first touched Trevor's strong neck, he jumped and she thought he might shoot straight through her ceiling. Talk about tense. The man was a walking time bomb. At this rate, he'd have a heart attack by age forty.

But it hadn't taken long for the uptight headmaster to relax. He'd melted under her touch like a stick of butter on a sizzling griddle.

Grandfather Lawrence had never understood Claire's desire to learn Swedish massage. He'd considered it just another crazy notion. Well, it didn't seem so crazy now. She had to find some way to keep the headmaster here until she persuaded him to hire her. And Swedish massage was more acceptable than tying him to the lamppost.

By the time she finished with Mr. Mathison, he looked like a different person. The frown lines had vanished from his forehead and his dark eyes looked serene.

"You could become a professional masseuse," he said, his voice surprisingly mellow. "Have you considered that option?"

"I'm a teacher," Claire said firmly.

He reached for his cup and took a sip. "Mmm. This tea's delicious. What kind is it?"

"It's a blend of relaxing herbs—chamomile flowers, peppermint leaves, ginger root, lemongrass, and hops. I mix it myself. If the massage didn't work out all your tension, the tea will finish the job."

He nodded and took another sip.

"I'm sure you're relieved to have filled the sixth-grade position," Claire said, dying to know if he'd hired someone.

"It's not filled, exactly. But I have a prospect in mind." He stood. "Thanks for the massage and the tea, Miss Jennings. Now if you'll excuse me, I must be going."

Claire's heart plummeted as she also stood and gazed again into those near-black eyes that now appeared relaxed and lazy. Almost romantic, she thought, then quickly chastised herself for having inappropriate thoughts about her new employer. But the headmaster still didn't know he was her employer. And he was preparing to leave.

"Are you sure you won't have another cup of tea?" she offered, desperate to keep him a little longer. But as he sauntered lazily to the door, she realized another cup might put him in a coma.

"No thanks. There's a steak at the Hereford House with my name on it."

She sighed. "Well, good-bye, Mr. Mathison. Thank you for returning my briefcase."

He smiled. "Good-bye, Miss Jennings. I wish you success in your teaching career."

Claire watched the headmaster stroll out to his shiny green Jaguar. Had she only imagined the premonitions? Had she lost her touch? She heard the Jag's starter whine but the motor didn't turn over. It whined a second time. Then a third.

Claire almost shouted "Hallelujah" when the headmaster climbed out of his car and ambled toward her. "I'm afraid I'm out of gas."

He meant the car, but he looked out of gas himself. She must have brewed the tea too strong. "I'll drive you to the service station," she offered. That would give her a little more time to convince the headmaster that she could capably teach sixth grade at the Brookshire School for Young Ladies.

"No need. I belong to the Ace Auto Club. They'll take care of it. May I use your telephone?"

"Certainly. It's in the kitchen." Claire led the headmaster into the house. He pulled a card from his billfold and went to make his call.

What could she do in the next few minutes to convince this man that she would make an excellent sixth-grade teacher? As she pondered that question, he rejoined her in the living room. "The auto club will be here in half an hour. May I have another cup of tea while I wait?"

"Of course," Claire said, uncertain if giving the headmaster more tea would help or hurt her cause. While she wanted him relaxed, he did have to be conscious.

Mr. Mathison slipped out of his suit coat, draped it carefully over a chair, then settled into her blue velvet recliner. "I've had this service for a year and never used it. Might as well get my money's worth."

Claire nodded and smiled. "Good idea."

After the headmaster drank two more cups of tea, Claire noticed he'd leaned his head against the chair back. When the telephone rang, she excused herself and went to the kitchen to answer it. After she finished a short conversation with a friend, she returned to find the headmaster sound asleep. So sound asleep that it frightened her.

She walked over to him to make certain he hadn't died in her recliner. She touched his neck gently, feeling for a pulse, holding her breath as she searched. An unexpected thrill moved through her body as she felt the smooth skin of the headmaster's neck and caught a whiff of his cologne—a woodsy, masculine fragrance. She'd first noticed it during the interview. When she located his steady pulse, relief flooded her.

She took this opportunity to study his tanned, angular face. Dark eyebrows accented a long forehead and his aristocratic nose had a slight hook that only added to his charm. His cheeks showed a hint of four-o'clock shadow.

When she was certain he was all right, she sat down on the couch and paged through a magazine, glancing periodically at the headmaster, who showed no sign of waking.

Half an hour later, she heard a truck pull up out front so she walked over and shook the headmaster's shoulder. "Mr. Mathison? The auto club is here."

He didn't move a single, well-formed muscle.

She tried again. "Mr. Mathison?"

Nothing. Claire picked up the Ace Auto Club card that he had laid on her coffee table and went outdoors.

A man climbed out of the service truck and approached her. "We got a phone call from a Mr. Mathison saying he ran out of gas."

The understatement of the decade, Claire thought. She pointed to the Jag. "That's his car."

"Is Mr. Mathison here?"

"He's in the house but he's fallen asleep. He's not feeling well."

She'd just told a blatant lie. The headmaster probably felt better than he'd felt in years.

Claire watched the young man fill the Jag's tank. When he finished, he said, "I need a signature. A wife's signature will do. Are you Mrs. Mathison?"

Now what? Well, someone had to sign for the work, and she was the only one awake. "Yes, I am," she said impulsively. Had her nose started to grow yet?

She took the form the young man handed her and scrawled MRS. TREVOR MATHISON on the dotted line, hoping she'd spelled it right. He gave her a copy of the receipt, climbed into his truck, and drove off.

Claire went inside and glanced at the clock. 7:30. She hadn't eaten supper and she knew the headmaster hadn't either. She checked him again, realizing that he looked so innocent now. So peaceful. There was no sign of the stern man who'd preached about the importance of strict discipline in the classroom. She openly admired his lean body, his masculine hands and carefully groomed nails. They'd shaken hands at the conclusion of the interview and even in her disappointment, Claire noticed how strong and solid Trevor Mathison's hand felt wrapped around hers.

"Your car is ready," she told the sleeping man. But she spoke softly. She had decided to let him rest. He was bound to wake up sometime and when he did, his car would be gassed and waiting. Besides, when he was fully rested, he might be more receptive to her campaign.

Claire laid the auto club card and receipt on the coffee

table, and, thinking Mr. Mathison would sleep better if his tie were looser, she carefully undid the knot. She gently removed his black leather shoes.

There. Now he looked much more comfortable.

Claire heated some chicken soup she'd made earlier in the week, and when she checked the headmaster at 10:00, he slept just as soundly as he had at 7:30. She covered him with an afghan, turned out the light, and went to bed.

A loud pounding on her front door startled Claire out of a dream. She sat up and peered out her bedroom window.

Grandfather Lawrence! He had an awful habit of appearing at the most inconvenient times. Not wanting to irritate him by keeping him waiting, she hurried to the door without taking time to grab her robe.

"Good morning, Claire," Granddad boomed. "Not dressed yet? Why, it's seven o'clock. You're missing the best part of the day."

As she ushered her grandfather into the living room, Claire saw him stop and stare. The headmaster! She'd forgotten all about him!

Trevor stood beside her recliner, shoeless, with his tie dangling. He was an extremely disheveled version of the man who had interviewed Claire less than twenty-four hours ago.

"What in tarnation are you doing here, Mathison?" Granddad demanded.

The headmaster looked positively shellshocked. "Mr. Lawrence, sir. I can explain."

Granddad crossed his arms and glared. "This better be good."

Claire looked back and forth between her furious grandfather and the embarrassed headmaster, painfully aware that she wore only her nightgown. Why hadn't she taken time to get dressed? But it didn't really matter. Neither of the stern men paid her the slightest bit of attention.

Trevor's tanned skin had flushed deeply. "You see, sir, I was interviewing Miss Jennings for the sixth-grade position at Brookshire."

"In her nightgown? Doesn't that seem a bit unethical?"

Granddad's face turned a deep shade of red and Claire realized that his blood pressure had probably zoomed into the danger zone. He'd already had one heart attack and she didn't want him to have another. Certainly not on account of her. "Please sit down, Granddad. I'll explain everything. It's not what you think."

Jacob Lawrence continued to stare daggers at the rumpled headmaster who stood stocking-footed, flustered, and at a loss for words.

When Granddad finally sank onto the couch, Claire breathed a relieved sigh and sat beside him. Trevor Mathison continued to stand beside the recliner that had betrayed him last night.

Granddad turned his attention to her. "Claire Elizabeth, you have some explaining to do. You've done some crazy things in your life, but finding you half-dressed with the Headmaster of Brookshire School is a very serious matter."

"It's all perfectly innocent," Claire defended. "You see . . ."

Granddad's countenance suddenly changed. He reached down and picked up the Ace Auto Club receipt lying on the coffee table. As he studied it, a smile spread across his face. "Well, well, well," he said, patting her hand. "There's no need to explain, after all."

He strode across the floor to where Mr. Mathison stood. Claire saw the headmaster shrink back when her grandfather extended his hand. "Looks like congratulations are in order, Mathison," Granddad said. "Why didn't you tell me you married my granddaughter?"

Chapter Two

"This seems pretty sudden," Granddad said, coming to sit beside Claire on the couch. "How long have you two known each other?"

Claire's palms grew sweaty as she realized that Granddad actually believed she and the headmaster were married. She'd better set him straight fast. "Not long at all. You see . . ."

"Ah, a short romance," said Granddad, who preferred talking to listening. "I can understand that. Your grandmother and I had a whirlwind courtship ourselves. A mutual friend introduced us and we were married six weeks later. Everyone said it would never last, but we proved them wrong." Granddad glanced at Mr. Mathison, who still stood dumbfounded beside the recliner. "Sit down, son. Make yourself comfortable."

The headmaster sank into the chair, probably wishing

it would swallow him up. He looked positively dumb-founded.

Claire sighed. Any minute now, Mr. Mathison would call a halt to this ridiculous charade. But since he didn't seem equal to it yet, she would try again. "You see, Granddad, I interviewed for the sixth-grade position at Brookshire School, and—"

Granddad slapped his knee. "Very clever, Claire. Very clever. You decided to beat me on my own turf."

"You don't understand," she said, determined to get the floor long enough to explain. "The headmaster interviewed me for the sixth-grade position, and—"

"—you fell head over heels in love," Granddad boomed. "Now, if you were nineteen, Claire, I would object. Strenuously. But you're turning thirty next month. I was afraid you planned to stay single for the rest of your life."

Claire cringed. Couldn't Granddad shout the news of her impending birthday any louder? There were probably a few people in the next block who hadn't heard him.

She shivered. Her nightgown only reached mid-thigh and she suddenly felt acutely aware of her state of un-dress. Granddad slipped his arm around her shoulders. "You're cold, honey. Run and get dressed, then I'll treat the newlyweds to breakfast."

This gross misunderstanding was gaining momentum at breakneck speed. Claire glanced from Granddad to her would-be husband, feeling desperate now, as well as cold. Finally, she ran out of the room in total frustration.

After slipping into a pair of jeans and a pink cashmere sweater, she hurriedly applied some makeup, then brushed her hair. She'd give the headmaster ample time to tell Granddad the truth. The whole ridiculous truth. Granddad would be disappointed, but it wouldn't be the first time.

When she returned to the living room, Mr. Mathison and Granddad were talking. Well, Granddad was talking—Mr. Mathison was listening.

Granddad turned to face her. "You look lovely, pumpkin. It seems marriage agrees with you."

She didn't know if marriage agreed with her or not. But she did know that her grandfather had not been set straight.

"I'm a little surprised, but doggone it, Claire, I couldn't be more pleased. I said for years that all you needed in your life was some real stability. And now you're a married woman." He shook his head. "I can hardly believe it."

"Neither can I," she said honestly.

"I was just telling Mr. Mathison . . ." Granddad paused. "Since you're now my grandson, I suppose I should call you Trevor."

The headmaster ran his finger around the inside of his shirt collar, as if he wasn't getting adequate oxygen to his brain. "I'd like that, sir," he croaked.

Granddad's smile was positively dazzling. "Now, where would you kids like to go for breakfast?"

The last thing Claire wanted to do was take this marriage out in public. It was hard enough to manage it in the privacy of her own home. "Why don't I fix some pancakes, instead. We'll go out another time."

Granddad nodded. "Fine with me. Trevor, your wife

makes the best pancakes in town. But I suppose you know that already."

It seemed strange to hear Granddad call the headmaster "Trevor" when Claire called him Mr. Mathison. "I'll go start the pancakes," she told them, glad to put some distance between herself and the two men. She'd just cleared the living room when she heard Granddad say, "Trevor and I will come along and watch."

More good news, Claire thought as the two most disciplined, strong-minded men on the planet followed her into the kitchen.

She started mixing pancake batter as Granddad and Mr. Mathison settled at the kitchen table. "Trevor, why don't you fix us a pot of coffee?" Granddad suggested.

The headmaster looked as if someone had just asked him to recite the alphabet backward. But he got up and walked over to the coffeepot, then waited for instructions.

"I bought a new can of coffee, Mr. . . . honey," Claire said, handing it to him. "The can opener's in the junk drawer on the far left." She looked at Granddad. "The kitchen isn't familiar territory to . . . to . . ." Good heavens, what should she call the man? Mr. Honey wouldn't do.

Granddad waved the comment aside. "I don't enjoy cooking much myself, son."

Claire saw a flush creep from below Mr. Mathison's rumpled shirt collar, making his tanned neck appear suddenly sunburned. Becoming an instant member of the family was causing him stress.

Her attempts to explain were getting her nowhere.

Why fight it? She might as well say what Granddad wanted to hear.

"So you kids just ran off and got married, huh? I suppose I should have expected this. Claire, you've always been impulsive."

The headmaster's eyes rounded in utter shock. Somehow he managed to pour water into the reservoir of the pot and measure out the coffee. His hand shook slightly which seemed incongruous for the disciplined man.

Unfortunately, the attraction Claire felt for Trevor Mathison hadn't dimmed a bit since yesterday. His slightly rumpled clothes and vulnerability added to his charm.

As the water gurgled into the coffeepot, Claire's pretend husband settled back at the table. She poured batter onto the sizzling griddle, glad to turn her attention away from these two men and this impossible conversation.

As the kitchen filled with the rich aroma of fresh coffee, Trevor tried to sort through the unbelievable events unfolding around him. He didn't hold much hope for salvaging this ridiculous scenario. The wacky Miss Jennings had tricked him into a sneaky scheme that could get him fired. All because he hadn't hired her to teach at Brookshire School.

And he'd thought his former fiancée was a free spirit. He'd known Claire Jennings less than twenty-four hours and she'd long since surpassed Jessica. Returning her briefcase, a simple gesture which should have taken half an hour of his time, had sent his life spiraling out of control.

"I suppose you two will move into Trevor's apartment," Mr. Lawrence speculated. "It's considerably larger than this house."

This has got to stop, Trevor thought desperately. And it looked like he was the one to set Jacob Lawrence straight. "Chairman Lawrence, sir," Trevor said, "I'm afraid you have the wrong impression."

"Oh? How's that?"

Now that Trevor had the floor, he wasn't quite sure what to do with it. What could he tell Jacob Lawrence? That the chairman's devious granddaughter had tricked him into a pretend marriage so she could meet the terms of the ridiculous ultimatum? That wouldn't help his case.

"For now, we'll probably stay in Claire's house," Trevor said, surrendering the war before fighting the first battle.

Mr. Lawrence nodded solemnly. "It would be more economical to live here. That way, the two of you can save for a bigger house."

Trevor didn't comment. A quote by Abraham Lincoln suddenly popped into his head: *"It is better to remain silent and be thought a fool than to speak and prove the same."* He'd take Lincoln's advice.

"I know the board has pressured you to marry, Trevor. We feel it looks better to have a family man at the helm of an all-girls school." Granddad chuckled. "But never in my wildest dreams did I think you'd solve that problem by marrying my granddaughter."

It had never crossed Trevor's mind, either.

Miss Jennings set a plate of steamy pancakes in the middle of the table. "Would you get the butter and syrup out of the refrigerator door, Mr. . . . Honey?"

Why did she keep calling him Mr. Honey?

Trevor did as she asked. In less than twenty-four hours, she'd turned him from a sensible, reasonable man, into a robot who did her bidding.

"What about a honeymoon? Will you kids have time for one?"

Miss Jennings blushed the same shade of pink as her sweater. When she didn't comment, Trevor assumed the next lie was assigned to him. "We don't have time for a honeymoon. I'm very busy getting ready for fall term, and interviewing for the sixth-grade opening has added to my workload."

Jacob Lawrence winked again. "I trust that position's been filled. You did have the good sense to hire Claire, didn't you?"

The moment of reckoning. Miss Jennings held her fork poised above the golden pancakes and studied him with those fascinating cornflower blue eyes.

She'd trapped him, all right. There was no escape. "Yes, sir. I had the good sense to hire your granddaughter."

Mr. Lawrence leaned over and slapped Trevor companionably on the back. "A good choice, son. And don't worry about that item in the bylaws stating married people can't be employed at Brookshire. I'll work it out with the board."

Trevor had to hand it to Miss Jennings. Her carefully crafted scheme worked. She had Jacob Lawrence convinced they were husband and wife. And Trevor knew without a doubt that if he tried to fire the chairman's granddaughter, or, heaven forbid, "divorce" her, his job would be history.

He glanced at his adversary. She didn't look like the conniving woman she was. *She actually looks sweet,* he thought. *And innocent.* He nearly laughed out loud at the incongruous thoughts. Innocent wasn't a word to describe this woman. Tricky, cunning, manipulative— those words fit.

Trevor choked down his last pancake and Jacob Lawrence glanced at his watch. "I'm meeting some of the board members for a game of golf. Want to join us, son?"

Trevor couldn't believe it. The Chairman of the Brookshire Board had just invited him to play golf! During the past year, Mr. Lawrence had barely acknowledged him. But he was upwardly mobile now that he'd "married" the chairman's granddaughter.

Trevor couldn't continue this charade. Certainly not at a golf game with Jacob Lawrence and other members of the board. "Thanks for the invitation, sir, but I've ... we've got things to do."

"I don't blame you for turning me down. If I was a new bridegroom I'd stay home with my lovely wife before I'd play golf with a bunch of old codgers. You're all right, Trevor. See me to the door, will you, Claire?"

That will give me a chance to tell Granddad the truth, Claire vowed. *And not a moment too soon.* She took his arm as they walked toward the entryway.

Granddad patted her hand. "I must admit that I didn't think you'd get your life on track before your thirtieth birthday, but you pulled it off. You could have done a lot worse than Mathison. He's a good administrator with a bright future." He shook his head. "And to think that next week, you'll begin your teaching career. Claire Elizabeth, you've made your old granddad mighty proud."

As she looked into her grandfather's eyes, Claire saw a deep sense of approval. How welcome it was. Suddenly, her resolve weakened. Maybe she'd wait a little longer before confessing. This bogus marriage was making Granddad incredibly happy. How could she tell him she was as single as ever with no prospects?

Feeling incredibly guilty, she kissed him good-bye and returned to the kitchen where the headmaster stood staring out the window.

He turned to glare at her, his black eyes icy. "Very clever, Miss Jennings. First you fill me with herb tea, next you let me fall asleep in your recliner, and then you convince your grandfather, who just happens to be Chairman of the Brookshire Board, that you and I are married. Very clever."

Claire felt blood rush to her face. "I only wanted to help you relax. When you came over here yesterday, you were tension personified. The massage and herb tea worked wonders. Why you actually turned into a human being—for a little while."

"And what was your motivation for relaxing me?" Trevor demanded. "To trick me into hiring you."

Ouch. The truth hurts. "I won't deny that I want the job. But that doesn't mean I'm not interested in your welfare. I am."

"Then, why didn't you wake me when Ace Auto Club arrived?"

"I tried. Twice. You were out like a light."

His dark eyes narrowed and she thought she saw sparks fly. "You should know. You drugged me."

The man was impossible! "Herb tea is not classified as a drug," she snapped.

Mr. Mathison stroked his jaw and looked pensive. "There's only one part I can't figure out. How did you make your grandfather think we are married?"

Claire felt so frustrated she couldn't say another word. She strode into the living room and the headmaster followed. Picking up the auto club receipt from the coffee table, she thrust it at him. "I couldn't wake you and the mechanic said a wife's signature would do. So I faked the signature. Who'd know the difference?"

"The Brookshire Board, for starters." Trevor sighed deeply. "I hope you realize that you've just destroyed my career."

The look of pain in Trevor Mathison's dark eyes lessened Claire's anger. "This doesn't have to hurt your career. Granddad thinks you're an excellent administrator. He just told me so."

The dark eyes narrowed. "And what will he think when he finds out our marriage is a hoax and that I haven't hired you for the sixth-grade position?"

"Granddad's extremely fair. It won't matter."

"It'll matter plenty. And things won't be so rosy for you either when he finds out."

He was right, of course. Claire sank onto the couch and Mr. Mathison settled in an easy chair, keeping a healthy distance from her treacherous recliner. She sighed deeply. "I guess we're both in trouble."

"Big trouble."

When he crossed one leg over the other and slipped off his tie, Claire couldn't help but notice that the headmaster was in very good shape. The man was nearly six feet tall and solid muscle. As he rolled up his shirt sleeves, she noticed his tanned arms. He ran a hand through his dark hair leaving one piece sticking straight up, reminding her of Alfalfa on "The Little Rascals." She almost chuckled but thought better of it. "We'd better figure a way out of this marriage."

He arched an eyebrow. "A way out?"

"Of course. You don't think for a moment that I'd marry you?"

"You have excellent motivation to do just that. It would please your grandfather and save your inheritance."

Claire glared at him. "No offense, but I'd rather be disinherited than become your wife."

Now he looked confused. "If this wasn't a scheme, why didn't you tell your grandfather the truth before things got out of hand?"

"Why didn't you?"

As Trevor gazed into those blazing blue eyes, some of his own anger drained away. One thing was clear: Claire Jennings was a beautiful woman. If he'd had any doubt about the extent of her good looks, seeing her this morning had alleviated them.

She crossed the long legs he remembered admiring yesterday and drummed her pink fingernails on the end table next to the couch. For several moments, they sat in awkward silence. Then she said, "Our conversation at breakfast was really awkward. I didn't know what to call you." She eyed him closely to see how he'd take her comment.

"How do you think I felt when your grandfather asked me to make coffee?"

She grinned slightly. "You probably felt out of your element."

He nodded. "You've got that right."

Funny, they were having a conversation. An actual conversation. Four exchanges and neither of them had accused the other of anything. "I've been called a lot of things," he ventured, "but never Mr. Honey."

Her lovely mouth curved into a big smile. She focused her blue eyes on him and he realized that he'd better watch himself. Miss Jennings attracted him more than he cared to admit.

"I'd like to ask you a question. Why didn't you hire me after the interview?"

"As I explained yesterday, this sixth-grade class is a tough group. They're the oldest girls at Brookshire and they flaunt their advantage. You seem . . ." How could he say this tactfully? "You seem too easygoing to take them on. I don't think that you and this position are a good match."

"If you'll give me a chance, I can prove what a good teacher I am."

He frowned. "I don't have much choice now, do I? I can't tell your grandfather that I've changed my mind."

Joy flooded her face. "You mean you'll hire me? To teach sixth grade at Brookshire?"

He was losing this battle fast, Trevor realized. "Why

don't we start on a trial basis? I'll have you sign a sub-stitute teacher's contract and in four weeks I'll evaluate your progress. If you're satisfied with the job, and if I'm satisfied with your performance, I'll draw up a perma-nent contract." He hated himself already, but saw no al-ternative.

Miss Jennings's pretty face beamed with pleasure and relief. "That sounds fair to me."

"Then it's settled. I'll run over to my apartment, take a shower, and bring the temporary contract by for you to read and sign. I'll be back about one o'clock if that's convenient."

"It's perfect."

"Now," he said pointedly, "the only thing left to settle is our marriage. We can't let this charade continue."

"After I sign the contact, I'll go to Granddad's and explain everything."

She made it sound simple but it wasn't. Mr. Lawrence wasn't a man to be toyed with. Trevor cringed, thinking of the colossal mess this woman had gotten them into.

As he drove the short distance to his apartment, his thoughts swirled in confusion. He reviewed the incidents of the morning, trying to make some sense of them. Was it possible that this scheme hadn't been preplanned? Had Miss Jennings told the truth when she insisted that all the events leading to the deception of Jacob Lawrence were an innocent hodgepodge of happenings? Like one out-of-control domino tipping and sending a line of them tumbling?

He parked the Jag in his driveway and entered the apartment. How different it was from Claire Jennings's place. The clean lines and open spaces gave his home a spacious, organized look. And his furniture contrasted starkly with Miss Jennings's eclectic clutter.

Trevor shed his wrinkled clothes, shaved, and took a hot shower. Then he slipped on a pair of jeans and a beige cableknit sweater and splashed on some cologne. After eating a bite of lunch, he hopped into the Jag for another trip to Mulberry Lane.

When Miss Jennings opened the door, Trevor felt his pulse quicken. Each time he saw this woman, she seemed more appealing than the time before. She led him to the kitchen table where they'd recently perpetrated fraud and they looked over the contract. Trevor leaned close, pointing out several clauses, and tried to ignore the delicate fragrance of her delicate perfume. When he'd finished explaining, she signed her name. CLAIRE ELIZABETH JENNINGS. The last time she'd signed a document, she'd written MRS. TREVOR MATHISON. He still couldn't believe the trouble that one impetuous gesture had caused.

"Everything's settled," he said. "You can come to school Monday morning and set up your classroom."

"Wonderful. Thanks for giving me this opportunity."

He slipped the signed contract into his briefcase and stood. "See you on Monday."

Claire realized she couldn't let Mr. Mathison go quite yet. After he'd left this morning, she'd spent more time meditating. Then she'd brewed up a new batch of tea and studied the leaves in the bottom of her cup. She'd gasped at their message.

So now she had to detain the headmaster once again. "Mr. Mathison? May I say something before you go?"

He sat back down, looking frustrated. "What is it now, Miss Jennings?"

She retrieved her cup from the kitchen counter and held it for him to see. "Just look at that."

"So? Rinse it out."

"There's a message here. A very clear message. Yesterday the tea leaves indicated I'd get the teaching position. I'd almost given up hope, but they were right."

"Miss Jennings, tea is for drinking. Books are for reading. Which reminds me, I have some textbooks in my trunk that you can start reviewing."

"I'd like that," she said. "But don't you want to hear the message?"

He sighed deeply. "I suppose so. What did the tea leaves say?"

"Marriage," she told him. "As plain as day."

He shot to his feet. "Marriage? Have you lost your mind?"

At that moment, the doorbell rang and Claire went to answer it. A delivery man handed her the largest bouquet of yellow roses she'd ever seen. "Are you sure these are for me?" she asked.

"Positive."

Claire thanked the delivery man and carried the armful of roses into the kitchen. "Aren't they gorgeous? I wonder who sent them?"

"Probably your boyfriend. He must be serious to send so many roses."

"I don't have a boyfriend. At the moment," she added. When she ripped open the small envelope, Claire's heart sank.

"Well, who are they from?"

She bit her lip. "You won't like it."

"Why would I care? I don't know any of your friends."

Claire cleared her throat. The card says 'Congratulations on your recent marriage.' It's signed: the Brookshire Board of Directors."

She glanced at Trevor who looked more horrified than ever. Claire swallowed hard. "And there's more."

"More?" he croaked.

She nodded. "The P.S. says, 'We're planning a wedding reception for you next Saturday evening at the Fairfield Country Club.' "

Chapter Three

"Can I get you some coffee, Mr. Mathison?" Claire asked, trying to soften the explosion of the most recent bombshell.

"Only if it's in a really big cup. One I can drown myself in."

"Don't say that. You shouldn't joke about suicide."

"What makes you think I'm joking?"

Was he serious? Claire wondered. She'd better keep an eye on him. He certainly was overloaded with stress. "I can clear up all this confusion," she said, trying to lift his spirits. "I'll go over to Granddad's right now and tell him the truth."

He sighed heavily. "What will you say? That we pretended to be married because it pleased him? That we tried to straighten him out but he wouldn't stop talking long enough to listen?"

37

"Yes. That's exactly what happened."

He shook his head. "It's too late for that. We'd both look foolish. We should have forced him to listen before things got out of hand."

He was right, of course. It would be impossible to explain now. Besides, Granddad had a short fuse when he felt manipulated. Claire realized that this dilemma could have serious repercussions for the headmaster as well as herself. "If you have any ideas on how to get us out of this mess, I'll gladly listen."

Mr. Mathison shook his head, looking more depressed than ever. "It would take the great Houdini to escape from this predicament. May I use your restroom, Miss Jennings?"

"Let me straighten the bathroom first."

"That's not necessary."

"Yes, it is." She hurried down the hall to the half bath, closing the door behind her.

After a quick perusal of the room, she decided nothing was out of place. She opened the bathroom door and found the headmaster waiting in the hall. She brushed past him. "It's all straightened. You can go on in."

Mr. Mathison entered the bathroom and closed the door. A moment later, Claire heard the water running.

Claire paced the narrow hallway, wondering if she should barge in and save Trevor Mathison from this mess.

Poor man. It was her fault he felt so hopeless. She had to find a way out of their dilemma. One that would allow the headmaster to save face. While the tea leaves indicated marriage, that was out of the question. But what about a pretend marriage? *Hmm. That might work.*

All was quiet in the bathroom. Too quiet. Claire leaned against the door hoping to hear a sound. Any sound. She felt her heartbeat accelerate as she wondered about his safety. If he didn't come out in the next thirty seconds, she'd have no choice but to go in after him.

Twenty-nine, twenty-eight, twenty-seven, twenty-six . . .

When the bathroom door opened, Claire lost her balance, and tumbled into the arms of the surprised headmaster.

He grabbed her and while it was merely a protective measure, his arms felt marvelously strong around her shoulders. For a moment, she leaned against him, taking in his masculine scent. "I'm terribly sorry," she said, struggling to regain her composure. "I . . . I was afraid you couldn't get out of the bathroom. You see, the lock isn't working properly."

Trevor stepped back and tried to tamp down the flood of emotions that engulfed him when Miss Jennings fell into his arms. She was muttering something about a broken lock on the bathroom door, but having her so near had him sidetracked.

He'd better get out of this loony bin fast. Just moments ago Miss Jennings had scurried out of the bathroom. Then the moment he opened the bathroom door, she'd tumbled into his arms.

He'd had to be alone for a few minutes and the bathroom seemed the only refuge. He'd had to think. When he was around Claire Jennings his ability to concentrate diminished considerably.

He'd splashed cold water on his face, trying to startle his brain back into working order so he could figure a way out of this craziness. But he hadn't come up with one feasible plan. If there was a solution to the runaway soap opera his life had become, he had no idea what it was.

"I think I have the answer to our problem," Miss Jennings told him when she was again standing on her own two feet.

He glared at her. "If it falls into the category of falsifying signatures, relaxation techniques, or fortune-telling, I'm not interested."

"It doesn't." She grabbed his arm and ushered him back to the kitchen table. He sat down, though he would have much preferred to barge out the front door, leaving Miss Jennings and Mulberry Lane far behind.

"Are you ready for this?"

"For more insanity? Sure. Dish it up."

Her eyes caught and held his. "We could pretend to be married."

He stared at her unable to fathom the suggestion.

"Just for a little while. Until we figure out a better plan. That would please Granddad and your job would be safe."

He gazed into her lush blue eyes. "Surely, you're joking."

She shrugged. "Do you have a better idea?"

He didn't.

"Where do you live?"

"On Manor Road. Three blocks from here."

"You can stay at my place in the evenings until it gets

dark. Then you can sneak back to your place. But you'd have to come back in the mornings, before sunrise. To keep up appearances." She leaned closer, her shiny blond hair brushing softly against his cheek. "What do you think?"

He shook his head. "It would never work." And it wouldn't. How could he possibly occupy this house, any house, with this gorgeous, impulsive woman?

But in spite of his better judgment, the idea began to take shape. "If we wanted to pull off a pretend marriage we would have to live together."

Her lush eyes grew big as saucers. "Live together?"

"It's the only way."

She seemed taken aback, but still determined. "Where would we live? Your place or mine?"

Trevor looked around Miss Jennings's cluttered kitchen and thought of his own sparsely but tastefully furnished apartment. It was considerably larger than her house, and would give them more space. But for the life of him he couldn't imagine taking this woman home. It was the only aspect of his life still intact. "Do you have a spare bedroom?"

She nodded.

"I could stay here for a few days. Until we figure out what to do."

She swallowed hard. "All right."

"I'll pack some clothes and come back after supper," he said, hardly able to believe he'd made the insane suggestion. "We won't have to spend much time together. If my car's in the driveway part of the time, people will get the picture."

She nodded. "I'll clean out the spare bedroom while you're gone."

"Don't go to any trouble."

Miss Jennings's cheeks were flushed again and she looked soft and appealing. If he'd wanted a pretend wife, he couldn't have found a lovelier woman anywhere. *But she's not hitting on all cylinders,* he reminded himself sternly. While he honestly believed that, it unnerved him considerably that she was the one who'd come up with a workable solution.

"I have a suggestion," she said softly. "If we're supposed to be married, we should call each other by our first names."

He swallowed hard. "All right. Claire."

When the headmaster said her name, a thrill of delight raced through Claire. "Trevor," she said, trying on his name for size. It felt strange, yet somehow familiar.

She'd better watch herself around this man—keep her heart in tow. Part of her wanted to run from him. He was as demanding and controlling as Granddad. But another part, that she couldn't seem to ignore, felt enormously attracted.

After he left, Claire went to change the sheets in the spare bedroom. Would this room work for the headmaster? Her bookshelves were stuffed with self-help books, and a statue of Buddha sat cross-legged in one corner of the room. Plump and smiling, he gazed into space. Would the headmaster mind sharing his room with Buddha?

Claire dusted and vacuumed the room, then went to the kitchen and steamed some vegetables for supper. The doorbell rang just as she finished eating. It must be her "husband." Taking a stabilizing breath, she hurried to answer the door.

Trevor Mathison stood on her front porch, looking serious but no longer depressed. He held a hanging clothes bag in one hand and gripped his briefcase in the other. Funny, the headmaster was able to keep track of his briefcase. He took it everywhere he went. Claire wondered if he even took it into the shower.

"Do you still want to go through with this?" He eyed her suspiciously, probably thinking she had a justice of the peace stashed in the closet who would marry them tonight while he slept.

"Of course. I'll show you to your room," she offered, feeling a little like a bell boy.

As Trevor followed Claire down the narrow hallway, the scent of his woodsy cologne again sent her heart racing. She pushed open the door to her spare bedroom— his room now—and they both entered. "I hope you'll be comfortable here."

As Trevor glanced around, the apprehension he'd felt about this move converted into dread. The room was less than half the size of his own spacious bedroom. And it was filled with a conglomeration of strange items.

Buddha stared at him from his post in one corner. A wooden carving of St. Francis of Assisi guarded another and a picture of Mother Theresa hung over the bookcase. Trevor scanned the jammed shelves, seeing such titles as *Stay Healthy with Aloe Vera* and *Vinegar Fixes Everything.*

Not true. Neither aloe vera nor vinegar could fix his

runaway life. And now he wished he'd encouraged Miss Jennings to clean this place up when she made the offer.

"I can manage," he said, vowing to stay out of this room as much as possible. If he arrived shortly before bedtime and left before breakfast, he'd hardly have to be here at all.

"I've stacked clean towels on your bed," Miss Jennings said. *Claire*, he reminded himself. They'd agreed to use first names, at least during their fake-marriage interaction. At school, they could be more formal.

He forced a smile. "Thanks."

"The bathroom is between our bedrooms."

Trevor noticed that she'd changed from the soft pink sweater she'd worn earlier into a bulky yellow sweatshirt. While he missed the sweater, Claire looked soft and cuddly. This woman stirred longings in him he hadn't experienced since Jessica.

He'd better watch himself. Not leave his heart in charge. "What time do you shower in the mornings?" he asked. "We'll need a schedule."

"A schedule? Why?"

"So we won't be trying to shower at the same time," he explained, then realized that his words hadn't come out right.

She flushed. "Why would we do that?"

If he couldn't explain the fact that they'd need to alternate time in the bathroom, how would he ever communicate with Claire regarding teaching methods and school policy? He took a steadying breath and started over.

"If you'll tell me what time you take your shower in

the mornings, I'll schedule mine accordingly." *There. That should be crystal clear.*

"I don't shower in the morning or any other time. I take baths."

This was insane. He felt like a Martian who'd just landed on the planet earth and couldn't communicate with the alien. Trevor had always prided himself on being clear and precise, and up until now, he'd had little trouble making himself understood.

He tried again. "It doesn't matter if you shower or bathe. What does matter is what time in the morning you want to take your bath."

She still looked perplexed. "I bathe at night. You know, I've never understood why people like to take showers. It's like a trip to the car wash. You pass through the spray and swish off the surface dirt. But a bath . . ."

She tucked a strand of shiny hair behind her ear and he realized that even her ears were pretty. A look of peace came over her lovely face. "A bath is more than a way to clean your body. It's a time to relax and release the tensions of the day."

Communicating with this woman seemed impossible. But at least he'd extracted the answer to his question. Miss Jennings—Claire—would bathe in the evenings, which would leave the bathroom free for him in the mornings. "I'll shower at six A.M. if that's all right with you."

"Of course, it's all right with me."

Claire scrutinized the headmaster in disbelief. The man was obsessed with organization. He even scheduled his showers! Next he'd be making a reservation to brush his teeth! Trevor Mathison already outshined Grandfather Lawrence in the compulsive department.

"I'll let you get settled now," she said, exhausted by this tedious conversation. "I'll be in the living room, if you need me."

Claire sat cross-legged on the living room floor, grateful to escape the strong-minded Headmaster of Brookshire School. He'd brought in a box of sixth-grade textbooks and as she pulled them out, she held each one reverently in her hands. History, English, science, geography, math. As she thumbed through the volumes, she wondered how she'd ever convey all this information to her students. But she felt incredibly excited at the prospect.

After studying all evening, Claire's mind reeled with facts and figures and her back felt stiff. A long, leisurely bath would help. She felt a little hungry and wondered if Trevor might be hungry, too.

Trevor. That sounded strange. Too personal for such a formal, disciplined man. But when he'd returned with the contract this afternoon, wearing jeans and a sweater, she'd realized he did have a private life. He'd looked more relaxed in casual clothes but every bit as handsome. What would it be like to discover the headmaster's personal side? Would he let anyone close enough to see it?

Her stomach growled and she went to fix a snack. Should she fix one for him, too? She'd never run a boarding house before and wasn't sure of her job description.

Trevor probably hadn't brought food along and he'd

never ask for anything. She thought of him down the hall, possibly starving to death. Last night she'd worried that he'd died in her recliner. Now she hoped he wasn't starving in the spare bedroom. The man was a lot of trouble!

In the kitchen, Claire stuffed celery sticks with cream cheese. Was the headmaster getting hungry? Maybe she should take him some. She nibbled while preparing the snack, then carried two plates down the hall. After placing one on the edge of the tub—she'd indulge while she soaked—she carried the other to Trevor's room and knocked.

"Come in."

His deep voice stirred her emotions. When she opened the door, she found him stretched out on the bed, surrounded by papers. He still wore jeans but he'd pulled off his sweater and it lay, neatly folded, on the dresser. His T-shirt molded to his muscular chest in a most appealing fashion. The man looked terrific stretched out on her spare bed. If Granddad did fire him, he could make a fortune modeling men's clothing.

"I brought you a snack."

He sat up and took the plate she handed him and his hand brushed hers in the process. A current of electricity zigzagged through Claire's body and she wished she hadn't brought the snack. Things were complicated enough.

He grinned. "This wasn't necessary. But thanks. I was getting a little hungry."

"I'm going to take my bath now," she said, unable to meet his gaze. "The only reason I mention it is because

I spend a long time in the bathroom." She cleared her throat. "Use the half bath, if you need it."

All this bathroom talk was making the pretty Claire Jennings uncomfortable, Trevor noted. He'd bail her out by changing the subject. "I'm going to visit my sister tomorrow. She lives in the country, about an hour's drive from Fairfield. So I'll be out of your hair all day."

Such luscious hair to stay out of, he thought, and wondered what it would feel like to run his fingers though those shiny strands.

"What should I tell Granddad if he stops by?"

"Tell him I wanted to inform my sister about our . . . our marriage. Tell him you had too much school preparation to come along."

"That sounds believable."

"I guess you'll be at Brookshire early on Monday to get the room ready for your students."

She brightened. "Yes. I can't wait."

"Stop by my office around eight-thirty and I'll show you your classroom."

"Thanks. I will." She turned and left the room.

What will Monday bring? Trevor wondered as Claire went to take her bath. He closed the bedroom door and returned to his work, crunching on the celery sticks she'd supplied. He'd have preferred a brownie with chocolate sauce but the celery didn't taste half bad. A few minutes later he heard music drifting from the bathroom. Dulcimer music. It sounded mystical. Downright eerie. Must be part of her unwinding process.

Trevor finished his work, change into his pajamas, and

crawled between the sheets of Claire Jennings's spare bed. His "wife" was right next door, soaking in the tub.

He tried not to picture the scene but couldn't help himself. No doubt Claire had a candle burning. He'd noticed a sweet scent when he'd gone to the half bath to brush his teeth. He hadn't been able to identify it then, but now it came to him. Jasmine.

The bathroom was probably misty and dimly lighted. And the lovely Claire was soaking in the scented water. Was her silky blond hair pinned on top of her head, revealing her slender neck and soft shoulders? He found himself carried away with imagining. Even the dulcimer music started to sound good.

Get a grip, Mathison, he cautioned, bringing his day-dreaming to an abrupt halt. *The only reason you're here in this tiny room with Buddha, St. Francis, and Mother Theresa is so you can keep your job—save your occupational neck. Don't let this wacky lady's strange ways affect you. You've always determined your course in life and pursued it relentlessly. Don't stop now.*

He fluffed the pillow and finally drifted off to the strains of the dulcimer.

Déjà vu, Claire thought as she followed Diane down the carpeted hallway to the headmaster's office. Fortunately, she hadn't seen Trevor at all yesterday. She had so much preparation to do for school that she didn't need to be worrying about him. Was he hungry? Was he alive?

She wasn't quite as nervous today as she'd been on Friday. She'd landed the job and that felt great. And today she'd eaten a healthy breakfast of fresh fruit, yogurt, and wheat cereal. She'd learned her lesson with the sinus medication.

Her goal was to stay in tiptop condition so she wouldn't miss a single day of the glorious school year stretching ahead. She planned to drop by the health food store on her way home and stock up on vitamins.

Diane stopped in front of the headmaster's door. "Mr. Mathison, Miss Jennings is here."

The headmaster sat behind the oak desk, as drop-dead gorgeous as ever. Perfectly groomed and pressed, every single black hair in place. No one would believe how he'd looked in her living room Saturday morning . . . rumpled, shoeless, and befuddled. If she'd snapped a picture then, she could bribe him with it, should the need arise.

"Come in, Miss Jennings." His deep voice sounded warm and appealing.

"Thank you, sir."

Claire realized she'd become "Miss Jennings" again. She'd better not slip up and call him Trevor here. Or, heaven forbid, Mr. Honey.

He stood and walked toward her. "I'll take you to see your classroom now."

As Claire followed him out of his office, he said, "This building houses the administrative offices and the secretarial staff. On the left are the mailboxes for our teachers. You'll be assigned one and you'll need to check in often for messages and memos. Your classroom is in Anderson Hall, named after Theodore Anderson, our school's founder. It's one of the oldest buildings on campus."

"How nice," Claire said, unbelievably excited.

Trevor opened the door and they left Mason Hall. The weather was warm for early September and the sun hid behind a heavy cloud cover. But that didn't dim Claire's enthusiasm in the least. As she and the headmaster walked toward Anderson Hall, Claire thought she might explode from sheer happiness. She'd reached her goal at last. She was a teacher. And what a wonderful place to teach.

Half a dozen stone buildings trimmed with dark wood shutters clustered on a grassy hillside on the quaint college campus. Carefully trimmed trees and shrubs gave the campus the impression of being lovingly cared for. Claire couldn't believe her good fortune.

They climbed the steps and Trevor opened the door for her, then led her down a wide hallway, and stopped in front of classroom number 105. Claire stepped inside and was greeted by the smells of chalk dust and the musty wood of ancient desks. It was a typical old-fashioned classroom, complete with slate blackboards and chalk rails that lined the room. The outside wall held a row of small-paned windows that cranked open. The ceilings were high. Very high. An American flag hung beside the door and lots of empty bookshelves and bulletin boards cried out for decoration.

Claire noticed the big oak desk at the front of the classroom. *Her* desk. She turned to the headmaster. "It's a wonderful room. I love it."

He nodded. "Glad you approve. I'll leave so you can give it some personality. It's pretty sterile at the moment."

"Not for long," she said.

Trevor didn't doubt that for a minute. He wondered what Claire would tack up on her bulletin boards and felt anxious as he considered the possibilities.

Most Brookshire students came from traditional backgrounds—families with old money to whom heritage and a conservative mind-set were comforting. How would Claire relate to those wealthy parents, some of whom were admittedly stuffy? Could she communicate effectively with them about homework, grades, and the progress of their progeny? Or would she have them meditating at PTA meetings?

"I'll see you later," he said, taking his leave. She hardly noticed, she was so enthralled with her classroom.

Trevor felt a little guilty about Claire's obvious delight. To be honest, he hadn't given her feelings much consideration throughout this mixed-up ordeal. He'd only hired her to save his own neck.

But had he saved it? Or just bought himself a little more time? Once Claire started teaching he'd have to deal with the reactions of her students, their parents, possibly even the board of directors. He sighed. Even Jacob Lawrence's influence could only stretch so far.

As Trevor returned to his office, his thoughts backtracked to Saturday evening. He thought again of the crowded spare bedroom where he now lived. And of the dulcimer music—with his pretend wife bathing in the next room. He could almost smell the jasmine, almost picture the gorgeous Claire soaking in the tub.

Living in her house might solve some of his problems, but it created others. Like his growing attraction to his new sixth-grade teacher. The feelings he had for her already stretched beyond an employer-employee relationship.

He sighed, realizing he'd better watch it or he'd get into more trouble. Or was that possible?

Chapter Four

Claire tried to force down a bowl of cooked wheat cereal and a container of yogurt. The first day of school would be both exciting and stressful and she must eat a healthy breakfast. But her stomach was rebelling again.

She heard Trevor in the entryway, ready to leave for school. He left each morning at 7:00 and didn't return until 10:00 P.M. Since she'd given him a front door key, she rarely saw him.

"Claire?" His voice echoed from the entryway. "Can I talk to you a minute?"

"Sure. I'm in the kitchen."

She heard brisk footsteps as he walked down the uncarpeted hallway. Suddenly he stood before her, wearing a gray sport jacket, navy slacks, and a crisp white shirt accented by a muted paisley tie. He looked perfect. Just looking at him was a pleasure.

"How about a cup of coffee?" she asked, and was surprised when he nodded and joined her.

As she poured him a cup, Trevor folded his hands and studied her across the table. "We've both been busy getting ready for school to start, but we need to talk." It was an ultimatum not a request. Granddad revisited.

"I've been swamped trying to get my classroom ready and lesson plans drawn up," she explained.

"And that's very important. But we have other issues that require our attention."

"You mean school policies and procedures. I want to learn everything I can about Brookshire and get the year off to a good start."

"That isn't what I'm referring to. I'm talking about the wedding reception the board is planning for us on Saturday night."

Claire felt as if someone had punched her in her already upset stomach. "There must be some way out of it."

He shook his head. "Plans are well under way. I ran into Josephine Noble, one of the board member's wives. She handles all Brookshire's social affairs." He cleared his throat and a flush darkened his cheeks. "Mrs. Noble wants to know what colors she should use to decorate the country club, and if the menu she's selected meets our approval."

A sense of panic welled inside Claire. "Oh, dear. What shall we do?"

"I told her to call you."

"Why did you do that? We just can't go through with this, Trevor. A wedding normally precedes a reception."

He frowned. "Thanks to you, everyone on the Brookshire Board thinks there has been a wedding. And word is spreading fast at school, as well. We have a decision to make. Whether to tell the truth and face the consequences or continue with this insanity."

Claire swallowed hard. "I don't know what to say."

"I'll get back early tonight so we can resolve this once and for all. Are you free at eight?"

"Yes," she told him, wishing there was some way to escape from the corner she'd painted them into.

Trevor drained his coffee cup. "See you at school."

Claire watched him walk out of the kitchen and heard the front door close behind him. She sighed heavily. Never had her emotions been pulled in more different directions. Excitement, fear, and attraction to Trevor all blended into a hodgepodge of confused feelings.

Today she would meet her new class of thirty sixth-graders which was excitement enough for anyone. Then tonight she must choose the colors and menu for her wedding reception—or confess there had never been a wedding.

Her stomach rebelled at the thought and she pushed her now-cold cereal aside. *Slay one dragon at a time*, she told herself sternly. She'd head for school and worry about the reception later.

Girls, girls, and more girls. They filed noisily into the classroom. The only things they had in common were their gender and the Brookshire uniforms—white blouses, red corduroy jumpers, white tights, and black-

and-white oxfords. They reminded Claire of a troop of car hops from Burger Delight.

There were short girls, tall girls, pudgy girls, and rail-thin girls who looked as if a breeze would send them scurrying for cover. There were platinum blonds with long curly tresses and raven-haired girls with short hair-cuts. One girl had the frizziest head of brown hair Claire had ever seen. She looked as if she'd been accidentally electrocuted.

Some of the girls had budding young figures; others would be mistaken for boys except for their A-line jump-ers. Some wore glasses, others experimented with makeup. A few looked confident, others shy, still others mischievous. *What have I gotten myself into?* she won-dered.

As they took their seats, the noise level reminded Claire of a huge waterfall tumbling from some unknown height, drowning any sounds in its wake. The bell rang but no one paid the slightest attention.

"Girls," Claire said loudly. No response. "Students," she shouted. Still nothing. They giggled and chattered as if they were attending a slumber party.

Claire gazed at them in utter frustration. Finally, she walked over to the bookshelf and pulled out a huge un-abridged dictionary. While she didn't like to abuse books, she couldn't think of any other way to capture their attention. She held the heavy book above her desk, then let it drop. *Craaaaack!* The dictionary hit her wooden desktop, echoing like the shot heard round the world.

The room grew instantly silent.

Claire picked up the dictionary and returned it to its spot on the shelf. "That's more like it. I'll give you plenty of time to talk later, but now it's my turn.

"Before I call roll, I'd like to introduce myself." She turned to the blackboard and wrote MISS JENNINGS in neat, well-formed letters.

Giggling rippled through the classroom and Claire turned to face her students. "Perhaps you'd like to tell me what's so funny?" She glared at the girl who giggled the loudest.

"That's not what we heard," the girl sassed.

"Oh? What did you hear?"

"We heard that you and Headmaster Mathison got married. If that's true, why is your name Miss Jennings?"

Thirty faces, many with smirks, stared at Claire in rapt attention. The room was dead still as the girls anticipated her response.

Struggling to provide a vague answer, she finally said, "I choose to go by Miss Jennings. Not all married women take their husbands' names. Not anymore." She glared back at the girls until their smirks faded. "Any other questions before I call roll?"

There were no more questions. Claire took attendance, then seated the girls in alphabetical order, hoping to break up any cliques. She spent the next hour distributing textbooks and discussing plans for first quarter. The noise level remained high and Claire had to break up an argument between the girl with the electrocuted hair and a redhead half her size.

At 10:00, the girls filed out of the room for gym class.

Claire sat at her desk, glad for a quiet moment to catch her breath.

She stared at the name she'd printed so carefully on the blackboard. She'd momentarily forgotten she was posing as a married woman and had been caught off guard by the girls' questions about her marital state. She'd saved the situation reasonably well. But the issue was far from resolved. Tonight she'd discuss it with Trevor.

What would they decide? Would it be easier to curtail this runaway marriage now? Before even more problems developed? In the short time she'd known him, Trevor Mathison had complicated her life in more ways than she could count.

It wasn't just the marriage mix-up. Having Trevor at her house changed everything. She never knew when he might come home and want to talk to her so she had to stay presentable at all times. No more lounging around in her nightgown in the mornings or letting the dishes go unwashed.

Trevor's magnetic presence affected every aspect of her life, both professional and personal. To make matters worse, the attraction she felt for the handsome headmaster intensified with each passing day.

Maybe confessing was the best game plan. Then she could get her house back. Maybe even get her life back.

As if she'd conjured him up, Trevor appeared in the doorway and her traitorous heart started skipping beats. "How's it going?"

"Just fine," she lied.

As he walked toward her the entire room seemed to

fill with his powerful presence. Just being around Trevor made Claire feel both happy and intimidated. He certainly lived up to his headmaster title.

He glanced at her name on the blackboard and frowned. "Miss Jennings, huh? I thought you might go by Mrs. Mathison."

"I told my students that lots of married women keep their maiden names," Claire defended.

He shook his head. "I never could understand why women do that. Two people live in the same house, sharing everything from toothpaste to toilet paper, but they go by different names. Crazy, if you ask me. If I ever marry, I'll expect my wife to take my name."

"Giving up your name isn't like turning in an overdue library book," Claire snapped. "It's sacrificing part of yourself. When two people marry, the man gets to keep the name he grew up with. But not the woman. Since ours is a pretend marriage anyway, why don't you take my name? Trevor Jennings, Headmaster." She chuckled. "Doesn't sound half bad."

He shot her an irritated glance. "If you want to go by Jennings, I couldn't care less. I didn't stop by to argue about names. I wanted to ask you to join me for lunch in the teachers' lounge. I always invite the new teachers to lunch on their first day of school."

"Fine," Claire said, still feeling annoyed with him but reminding herself that he was her principal and her teaching future rested in his hands.

"We can meet in the cafeteria at eleven-thirty, get our trays, then go to the teachers' lounge. The cafeteria's in

Raymore Hall, right next to Mason," he said. "How did you get along with your students this morning?"

"Just wonderful. The girls are terrific," Claire said, stretching the truth until she thought it might snap in two.

He looked. "Glad to hear it. "See you at lunch."

Claire watched Trevor leave again. He was always leaving and she was usually glad to see him go.

Despite the attraction she felt for him, this man set her on edge. Made her defensive. But she had to get along with him. She'd do anything to succeed at this job. She loved teaching and did want to please Granddad.

Now, it seemed, she had another man to prove herself to. And if she didn't please Trevor Mathison, he had the power to fire her.

She would somehow manage the job-related stress but this marriage scheme was killing her. All the pretense and half-truths were exhausting. She'd have put an end to it long before now if it wasn't for Granddad.

He'd looked so pleased last Sunday morning. Jacob Lawrence was a tough man to satisfy and she was finally meeting his expectations. While she didn't think she could keep up the deception much longer, did she really have the courage to set the record straight? And live with Granddad's displeasure?

Trevor scanned the cafeteria looking for Claire. When she came in he admitted, grudgingly, that she looked terrific. Her blond hair shimmered around her shoulders and the blue-gray tailored suit, white blouse, and navy pumps flattered her attractive figure.

She spotted him across the cafeteria and waved and

as she came toward him, he felt a distinct pleasure in watching her move. She walked with sure steps and quiet grace. To see her now, no one would guess that she looked to tea leaves for guidance.

They met in the teachers' lunch line. "I'm starving," she declared. "I was too nervous to eat breakfast."

"That's what you told me Friday at the job interview."

It was only five days ago but seemed an eternity. Long enough to disorder the life he'd so carefully constructed. He tried to stifle his resentment.

After they filled their trays, Trevor led Claire down the hall to the one room that offered teachers a brief respite from their students. When he walked in, Claire directly behind him, all eyes centered on them. Cindy Lewis, a fifth-grade teacher, said, "Welcome, Mr. and Mrs. Mathison." Everyone cheered and clapped and Trevor nearly dropped his tray from utter shock. He'd suspected the news of their "marriage" would spread quickly but not this quickly.

Coach Smith scooted down a place so the two of them could sit together and Trevor noticed Claire's cheeks flushed slightly. When they got settled, Cindy said, "I teach fifth grade next door to you, Mrs. Mathison. I'm Cindy Lewis. Welcome to Brookshire."

Trevor jumped again at the words "Mrs. Mathison" and Claire's cheeks turned a most becoming pink. "Thank you," she said. "But please call me Claire. Mrs. Mathison sounds so . . . so formal."

And so absurd, Trevor thought.

"When did you two get married?" Coach Smith quizzed.

"A week ago Saturday," he lied, wishing he didn't have to endure another grilling on the marriage that wasn't.

"Did you have a small wedding?" Cindy asked Claire.

Claire choked on a carrot stick and it took her a minute to catch her breath. "We went to a justice of the peace."

"Have you had any showers?"

Cindy, always aggressive and persistent, just wouldn't quit. Claire caught Trevor's eye and he saw panic on her pretty face. "No," she said. "But that's no problem. We have everything we need."

Cindy brightened. "But every couple needs a shower. Besides, I'd love to throw one."

"And I'll help you," added Betty Johnson, the kindergarten teacher.

"Let's do it soon," Cindy suggested. "How about next Tuesday evening at seven?"

"Trevor?"

Claire frantically grabbed his arm, setting all his nerve endings on alert. She'd only touched him a few times, but each time he'd felt warmth spread through him. Her cheeks continued to hold that becoming rosy glow.

"Do we have any plans on Tuesday evening?" She sounded desperate and her eyes held a pleading look. Claire Jennings wanted to be rescued.

For the first time since they'd met, Trevor was in a position of power and it felt good. "No plans at all, honey. Tuesday evening sounds fine." As he patted her arm, Claire's pleading gaze turned to censure.

Let her suffer, Trevor thought, feeling some satisfaction that his pretend wife was as miserable as he. *Maybe next time she'll think before she signs a name that doesn't belong to her.*

His orderly life had converted to one steady whirlwind of chaos. Trevor felt unbelievably annoyed with the beautiful woman beside him who sat chatting with his teachers. She had disrupted every aspect of his daily life.

After all, Brookshire School was his territory. His personal domain. And he'd been doing quite well until the day he interviewed Jacob Lawrence's granddaughter. Then, all the structure he'd worked so hard to put in place—both at school and in his private life—began slipping through his fingers like elusive grains of sand.

He'd bring a halt to it immediately but that was courting disaster. The board wanted him married, and admitting that he wasn't would cripple his credibility. And if that wasn't enough to destroy him, Chairman Lawrence could easily finish the job.

8:00. Claire heard the key turn in the lock. If nothing else, Trevor was prompt. She could set her second hand by the man.

He entered the living room where she sat on the floor surrounded by textbooks. "Hi," she said, still upset with him for refusing to help her get out of the wedding shower.

He sank onto the couch. "Looks like you survived your first day of teaching."

"Yes, I did," she said smugly. Not well, but he didn't have to know that. She wouldn't confess that Amy Jones put a frog in her desk drawer. Or that she'd screamed when it hopped onto her desk. And she wouldn't bring up the fact that several girls had answered roll call with the wrong names, confusing her beyond belief. She still didn't know if the girl with the electrocuted hair was Angela Jones or Kelly Freeman.

Claire scowled at Trevor. "Why didn't you rescue me at lunch today? You could have said we had other plans for Tuesday evening."

"Like you rescued me when your grandfather walked in Saturday morning?" He sighed. "I considered it, but Cindy would have pestered you until you set another date."

She sighed. "I suppose you're right."

"We're at a crossroads, Claire. This is our last chance to stop this runaway marriage."

"I know we'd both be happier if we confessed. But I hate to consider the consequences."

He nodded solemnly. "I'd probably have to resign. And it will be impossible to find another position with school already in session."

Claire felt a wave of genuine concern for her new principal. While she had a lot to lose by ending this charade, Trevor had an established career at stake.

She stood and went to sit beside him on the couch. "I wish I could go back and change that silly signature. That's what started this whole misunderstanding."

Trevor shook his head. "I can't pretend it's all your fault, Claire, much as I'd like to. I didn't try very hard to set the record straight."

It was the first time Claire heard Trevor admit he'd made a mistake. The touch of humility in his voice both surprised and pleased her. She turned toward him. "I'm sorry about all the trouble this has caused you."

He reached out and stroked her cheek. The tender gesture took Claire's breath away. His touch mesmerized her and sent tingling sensations scurrying through her. As he studied her with those intense dark eyes, his gaze cemented her to the couch. She didn't think she could move if the house caught fire. Trevor's scent filled her with yet another pleasurable sensation and she already had more than she could handle.

He leaned closer, his lips so near she could almost taste them.

He's going to kiss me! The thought fogged Claire's brain and put her emotions on overload.

She braced herself for the moment when Trevor's lips would touch hers. Just as she was about to turn loose of reason, to welcome the magic she knew his kiss would contain, the shrill ring of the telephone intruded.

With great difficulty, Claire pulled away from Trevor and got up to answer the phone. Her knees felt as weak as if she'd been in bed with the flu. She hoped to find her voice before she picked up the receiver. "Hello," she whispered, painfully aware of her breathy voice.

The woman announced herself as Josephine Noble. She was calling about the wedding reception and what colors she should use to decorate the country club.

Claire tried to suppress her mounting anxiety and speak politely. "Oh, yes, Mrs. Noble. Trevor said you'd spoken to him about the reception. Would you hold on a moment, please?"

Trevor had already reverted from a tender man who

sent Claire's senses reeling into the stern Headmaster of Brookshire. The Jekyll-Hyde transformation took just seconds.

He began pacing but had difficulty because her text-books created an obstacle course. "Mrs. Noble wants to know about the reception," Claire whispered, her feelings of dreaminess replaced by utter dismay. "Shall I tell her the truth?"

Trevor looked like a trapped animal. "Why didn't you ask my opinion earlier? When it would have made a difference?"

Claire glared at him. She returned to the phone, deciding she would handle this herself. And she'd be honest. It was the only way. The moment of truth was painful but she had to face it.

Just as she was ready to confess, Granddad's face flashed before her. Stern, demanding, disproving. And this disappointment would be a major one. It could end their relationship.

"Mrs. Noble? If you'd like to use peach and ivory for the decorations, that would be lovely."

Trevor's pacing accelerated and he stubbed his toe on her world atlas. He mumbled something under his breath she was glad she couldn't hear.

"The menu sounds wonderful," Claire told the woman who was rambling on about grilled salmon and new potatoes. "We trust your judgment entirely. Yes, seven o'clock will be fine. Trevor and I appreciate all you are doing for us."

Claire dropped the phone onto the cradle and turned to face Mr. Hyde. "I hope you like grilled salmon and new potatoes. That's what Mrs. Noble will be serving at our wedding reception!" She didn't know whether to laugh hysterically or run screaming out of the house.

Trevor looked as if he might spontaneously combust. He seemed as frustrated as he had the morning he'd awakened to Granddad's fury. He stood and squared his shoulders. "I guess we've decided to continue with this ridiculous charade. Good night, Claire." He turned on his heel and marched off toward the spare bedroom.

Claire sank into the recliner, where the nightmare had begun. She'd made some serious mistakes recently, starting with trying to meet the terms of Granddad's ultimatum. Now it wasn't just Granddad imposing restrictions. Trevor Mathison had joined the party.

She leaned back in the recliner, feeling more stressed than she'd felt in years. She tried to relax her taut muscles but couldn't manage it. She'd better meditate a while to clear her mind of all the confusion.

Forcing herself to be single-minded, she tried to reach a state of nirvana by releasing all her anxious thoughts. As they started slipping away, something else took their place. Thoughts of Trevor kicked in!

She remembered how he'd leaned toward her, remembered the longing she'd seen reflected in his magnificent eyes. The memory sent her pulse racing. How could a man who made her so angry, who frustrated her beyond belief, send her emotions lurching out of control?

The Headmaster of Brookshire had disrupted every facet of her life and was now interfering with her ability to meditate. Claire jerked the handle on the recliner, bringing it to an upright position. She picked up a magazine and fanned her face, welcoming the rush of air.

Meditation wouldn't help tonight, that was certain. Only one thing could help. While it was against her principles, she must have a shower. A long, cold shower.

Chapter Five

Claire checked her image in the full-length mirror. The ivory linen dress, edged with wide cotton lace, looked becoming. She stretched to pull the zipper the rest of the way up but it snagged in the fabric and her efforts only managed to lodge it more securely. A few more desperate attempts convinced her she couldn't fix this by herself.

Much as she hated to, she went to Trevor's room and knocked. He answered, dressed in tux pants and an ecru ruffled shirt. The man always looked terrific, but this was ridiculous. Claire's palms grew sweaty and her throat felt suddenly parched. "My zipper's stuck," she said.

A slight frown creased his brow. "Turn around and I'll dislodge it."

She turned, lifting her hair off her neck, and waited while he tugged and pulled, all the while holding her

70

breath so she wouldn't be mesmerized by his woodsy cologne. Several minutes dragged past as Trevor continued to fumble. Claire tried hard to ignore the pleasure of even this casual contact but in spite of her efforts, his warm fingers sent delicious shivers down her spine. After a light-year or two, he finally dislodged the imbedded zipper.

"There." She felt him secure it, then fasten the small hook and eye on the neckline of her dress.

She turned to face him. "Thanks. This is the only dress I own that will work for a wedding reception."

"I like it. You look . . ." He hesitated. "You look like a bride."

Approval sparked in Trevor's dark eyes which was a new experience. Her pretend husband didn't sanction her eating habits, her discipline methods, her practices of meditation or consulting tea leaves. To summarize, Trevor disapproved of her entire lifestyle.

The anxiety she'd experienced all morning suddenly built to major proportions. "Do you really think we can convince the board that we're married?"

He ran his hand through his hair. "We'd better. If they find out the truth, we'll both be job hunting. And for years to come, people will talk about the crazy headmaster and sixth-grade teacher who tried to pull off the biggest farce in Brookshire history." He chuckled sardonically. "We'll be notorious—like Jesse James."

Claire sighed. "That's not the kind of recognition I want. I'd settle for being a good sixth-grade teacher."

Claire would have better luck robbing trains like the James gang, Trevor thought grimly. From what he'd seen, she showed none of the earmarks of a good teacher. Too easygoing, and more than a little bit flaky, Claire was out of touch with reality. And if reality ever came home to roost, it was in a classroom of overactive twelve-year-olds who wanted to rule the world.

"I'll finish getting ready and meet you in fifteen minutes," she told him.

"Fine." He went back into the cluttered bedroom to put on his bow tie. By leaning closer to the mirror that hung over Claire's shelf of self-help books, he finally managed to get the tie in place.

He hadn't worn a tux since he'd been fitted for one a month before he and Jessica were to be married. He'd been ecstatic about their future together. Jessica was impulsive, happy, and in love with life. She "sat easy in the saddle of life," as Will Rogers so aptly put it. That's why Trevor couldn't believe it when he went to Jessica's apartment one afternoon and found a note taped to her front door.

Trevor:

I just can't go through with the wedding. We're too different, you and I. I've dated Ron a few times and he and I have so much in common. We've decided to spend the summer together in Mexico.

It would never have worked for us, Trevor. I'm genuinely sorry.

Jess

That note changed Trevor's life. His world crumbled when he read it and nothing had been the same since.

He'd telephoned Jessica's parents to be sure it wasn't a prank. It would be just like Jess to pull a silly stunt like that. An April fool kind of thing. But her mother verified the awful truth.

Claire reminded him a lot of Jessica. Warm, loving, impulsive, and not quite in touch with reality. That made him nervous. He forced the sad memories out of his thoughts. He had all the trouble he could manage without dredging up his painful past. Right now, he had a wedding reception to attend.

His own.

"What do you think, St. Francis?" he asked, consulting the statue of the monk who had supposedly discovered what peace and tranquillity were all about. *Is there a chance in . . . in Heaven that we can pull this thing off?*

Trevor squared his shoulders, then headed for the living room where Claire stood waiting. The ivory dress, which tastefully accentuated her figure, was perfectly suited to the occasion. She was being "appropriate" again. That always surprised him.

She'd swept her lovely blond hair on top of her head and pinned in some lilies of the valley. The neckline of the dress showed just enough to be fascinating, and the scent of jasmine drifted delicately around her. If he'd had to pick a pretend wife, he could have done a lot worse than Claire.

"Ready?" he asked.

Her lips curved into a small pout and for a moment he wondered what it would be like to kiss her.

She shrugged. "I doubt if I've ever been less ready for anything in my life."

They left the house and Trevor helped her into the Jag. He slid behind the wheel but before starting the motor, he reached in the backseat, picked up a florist's box, and gave it to her.

Claire's eyes lit with pleasure as she lifted out the corsage of peach-colored roses. "They're lovely, Trevor. How thoughtful of you to get me flowers." Her smile faded as quickly as it appeared. "I didn't get you a boutonniere."

"No problem. I bought myself one." He reached for a smaller box and pinned a single rose to his lapel.

Claire struggled to secure the flowers to her dress but wasn't getting very far. "Here. Let me help."

He leaned toward her and tried to fasten the corsage without doing her bodily harm. The pin looked positively deadly. It could double as a fencing foil.

As he pinned the flowers to Claire's dress, the jasmine fragrance mingled with the scent of the roses, attacking his senses like a double-barreled shotgun. Claire's nearness in the close confines of the Jag made matters worse.

He was getting ideas again. Crazy ideas. Like, what would it feel like to nuzzle that beautiful neck of Claire's? Or bury his face in that shiny hair? Or, better yet, kiss the mouth he'd almost succumbed to the evening Mrs. Noble called about the wedding reception?

"Ouch!" The point of the pin pierced his finger, drawing blood.

"Here. I've got a tissue." She dug in her purse and handed him one.

He blotted his finger, amazed that such a small prick could draw so much blood. But the stabbing had been well timed. The other evening, the telephone saved him from kissing his pretend wife. Tonight it was a florist's pin. He'd take any diversion he could get.

As they drove the distance to the country club, Claire's stomach started an insurrection the likes of which she'd never before experienced. When they reached the parking lot, she thought she might be sick. She breathed deeply, employing the calming breaths that she'd mastered in yoga class. That relaxed her enough so that she could get out of the car, put one foot in front of the other, and propel her body forward to her execution.

It only feels like an execution, she reminded herself. *It's actually a wedding reception.*

And these were civilized people. Even if they learned the truth about her and Trevor, they wouldn't string her up like a common criminal. After all, the only thing she'd murdered was the holy state of matrimony.

But if the truth came out, it would mean humiliation—for herself, for Trevor, and worst of all for Granddad. He'd be a laughing stock. That would paralyze his effectiveness as Chairman of the Board of Brookshire School and end her relationship with him forever.

Trevor led the way to the Rose Room and when they entered the exquisite room, complete with its heavy brass mirrors, massive crystal chandelier, and deep pile carpeting, everyone turned to stare at them. Then everyone clapped. Claire felt like the worst kind of impostor.

A woman in a pink linen suit came toward them. "Good evening, to you both. Mrs. Mathison, I'm Josephine Noble."

"It's nice to meet you." Claire wished the woman's last name was something other than noble. It added salt to the wound.

Mrs. Noble beamed at them. "We're so pleased our headmaster has finally married. And you're such a beautiful bride."

"Th . . . thank you," Claire stammered, feeling her neck get hot. She hoped she wouldn't turn blotchy. When she was nervous, she sometimes developed big red spots.

She glanced down and saw light-pink splotches appearing on her upper chest. Stage one. Well, it served her right. Sort of like having the letter A plastered on her chest.

But unlike Hester Prynne in *The Scarlet Letter*, no one could accuse her of adultery. She hadn't even kissed her new "husband." All he'd done was touch her cheek and zip her dress. But the thought of those two casual encounters made Claire's heartbeat accelerate.

"I thought we'd form a receiving line so everyone can speak with you personally, Mrs. Mathison."

"Please call me Claire."

Mrs. Noble smiled. "A pretty name for a pretty woman."

Claire flushed, which probably turned the blotches neon. And her stomach was now doing mutinous somersaults. If nothing else betrayed their secret, her body would shout it to the world.

At that moment she saw Granddad enter the Rose Room. He came over to hug Claire and shake hands with Trevor. "Ah, the bride and groom. How's my favorite grandson this evening?"

"Um, fine, sir. Just fine."

Claire noticed several beads of moisture neatly lined up on Trevor's forehead. The man even perspired in an organized fashion!

"Good evening, Jacob," said Mrs. Noble. "Everyone's dying to meet your lovely granddaughter so I've asked the newlyweds to form a receiving line. Would you join them?"

"I'd be proud to," Granddad boomed, and Claire thought she saw the massive crystal chandelier above them shake from the volume of his voice. Mrs. Noble shuffled them into place, putting Granddad first in line.

Claire sighed. Here she was again, sandwiched between the two most disciplined men on the planet. She felt as trapped as if she'd been handcuffed to a post, or secured in wooden stocks and displayed on the village green.

Mrs. Noble beckoned to the guests and the first couple approached Granddad. "Good evening, Fred, Liz," Granddad said. "I'd like you to meet my granddaughter, Claire Jennings Mathison. Claire, these are the Johnsons. Fred serves with me on the Brookshire Board."

"How do you do, Mr. and Mrs. Johnson?" Claire tried to ignore her unsteady voice.

Mr. Johnson bowed gallantly. "Good evening, Mrs. Mathison. We'd heard our headmaster had married, but didn't know what a lovely and gracious bride he'd selected."

Claire glanced down shyly and noticed that the blotches had progressed to stage two: shocking pink.

Granddad introduced her to Stanley and Margaret

Ward. "It's a pleasure to meet you, Mrs. Mathison," Mr. Ward said. "We hear you're teaching sixth grade. You'll give Brookshire a little class. High time, if you ask me."

"Why, um, thank you."

"May I see your wedding rings?" Mrs. Ward asked. "I just love brand-new diamonds. They catch the light so magnificently." She glanced down at Claire's left hand, which was naked as a newborn babe. "Oh, I'm sorry. I shouldn't be so nosy."

"The rings are being sized," Trevor volunteered. "And when Claire gets them back, you'll be the first one to see them, Mrs. Ward. That's a promise."

All traces of embarrassment vanished. "How wonderful," Mrs. Ward cooed. She turned to Claire. "You're a lucky woman to have such a gallant and handsome husband."

Claire nodded and forced a smile. Before the reception line ended, she had been asked the date of their wedding, which Trevor miraculously invented, if they had wedding pictures to show, and when they planned to have their first child. The baby question came from the mother of a board member. She was very old and probably figured she could ask anything she wanted.

Finally, the line ended and Claire glanced around the room. The reception hall was filled with round tables covered with ivory linen, then overlaid with tablecloths of peach lace. Silk flower arrangements in peach and ivory served as centerpieces and the tables gleamed with silver and crystal. At any other time, Claire would have delighted in the elegance. But tonight, it proved just another painful reminder of her fraudulent life.

Mrs. Noble surfaced and ushered them to the head table. When they were seated, Mrs. Noble announced that her husband, Ernest Noble, would propose a toast.

Claire couldn't believe the man's name was Ernest Noble. If God was trying to point out the error of her ways by surrounding her with people with moral-sounding names, he could have been more subtle. She wasn't stupid.

Ernest Noble took the toast seriously. He rambled on about the blissful state of matrimony, its rights and privileges—none of which remotely affected Claire and Trevor. He finished by wishing them a long, happy life and a houseful of children. Claire glanced at Trevor and thought he'd turned blotchy, too.

The waiters began serving dinner. The plate of grilled salmon, new potatoes, and steamed broccoli the waiter placed before her turned Claire's stomach. If she took a single bite her stomach would revolt.

So she sipped the drink in her stemmed goblet, trying to put off eating as long as possible. The light-pink beverage had a zing to it. It must be a wine punch. While she didn't usually drink wine, it might help her relax. She took another sip and felt the tickle as it slid down her throat.

Trevor seemed to be enjoying his salmon. The man must have a cast-iron stomach. Or maybe he didn't feel as if he'd committed treason. Claire drained the beverage in her goblet and a waiter came to refill it. By the time she was halfway through the second glass, her stomach began to settle and she managed to choke down a few bites of dinner.

"How are you doing?" Trevor whispered.

"I'm still alive. Do I get points for that?"

"I'd say surviving this evening is a major accomplishment. Once dinner is over, the only thing left will be the dance."

"The dance? You mean we have to dance, too?"

"Mrs. Noble tacks a dance onto the end of any social gathering."

"How much torture can a person be expected to endure in one evening?"

"Two persons," he corrected. "You're not suffering alone."

That was true. It was comforting, in a warped sort of way, knowing Trevor was just as miserable as she.

But in spite of his discomfort, her pretend husband looked breathtakingly handsome. His dark hair shined like the satin trim on his black tuxedo. Once again, every hair lay perfectly in place. Claire remembered how rumpled Trevor had looked the morning Grandfather Lawrence jumped to the wrong conclusion and forced them into this pretend marriage. A shotgun held to Trevor's head couldn't have worked more effectively.

Trevor looked too perfect. She reached for her goblet, and as if in fulfillment of her thoughts, accidentally knocked it over. The pale pink liquid raced down the tablecloth—straight for Trevor!

He shot out of his chair but not fast enough. One leg of his tux pants got soaked. Grandfather Lawrence and Mrs. Noble donated their napkins to the cause and Trevor mopped up as best he could.

He looked annoyed as he headed for the men's room,

the trouser fabric clinging to his leg. Well, he didn't look quite so perfect now.

When Trevor returned, he seemed more somber than ever. Claire wished she'd doused herself rather than him but the liquid had a mind of its own. "I'm sorry," she said.

"Forget it."

When the waiter served them a frothy ambrosia topped with whipped cream, Claire decided not to push her stomach past its limits. She offered her ambrosia to Trevor, who happily accepted.

Some eating habits the man had. He hadn't touched his broccoli. And he'd eaten very few of the new potatoes. But he'd managed two desserts. Make that three. Josephine Noble had just donated hers, as well. Trevor's sweet tooth knew no bounds.

As Claire watched the band set up on the polished parquet floor nearby, she realized that the next form of punishment was about to begin. The band members tuned their instruments, then started playing old love songs. Very old love songs. Mrs. Noble must have hired the band.

Ernest Noble stood and tapped his spoon on his water goblet. "Ladies and gentlemen, may I have your attention please?"

Was he going to continue his dissertation on wedded bliss? That was cruel and unusual punishment and Claire didn't think even *she* deserved it. The Rose Room turned suddenly quiet. "My wife Josephine has arranged for The Dream Makers to play for our newlyweds tonight," Mr.

Noble said. "We'd like the bride and groom to dance the first dance alone. Then we'll join them on the floor."

Claire sat frozen in her chair. Was there no end to the humiliation? And to make matters worse, people were clapping again. She'd never been clapped for in her life until the last few days. Now it had become an epidemic.

She glanced desperately at Trevor. Did his controlled expression mask the same kind of panic she was feeling?

He stood and pulled out her chair. "May I have the pleasure, Mrs. Mathison?"

If his voice hadn't been edged with sarcasm, it might have been a touching moment.

Claire stood and let him escort her to the dance floor as the band played "The Sweetheart of Sigma Chi." Claire recognized the ancient song because she'd listened to Granddad's tapes as a child.

They reached the dance floor and Trevor pulled her into his arms. A little gruffly, she thought, but her body molded to his surprisingly well. Trevor's nearness proved as delectable as Claire had imagined it would be, and his woodsy scent consumed her senses. She'd learned to dance while in Europe and quickly realized that Trevor could dance, too—smoothly and with a polished grace.

Trevor had often heard this song played at Brookshire parties. It had become a theme song for the gentlemen on the board. The lyrics spoke of golden hair, like Claire's. And blue eyes. Like Claire's. The song seemed written for the lovely lady in his arms.

Claire's gorgeous blue eyes seemed tinged with fear.

Make that panic. But was there more than panic in those stunning eyes? Did he see longing there, as well?

He'd never seen a woman that nature had been more generous to than Claire Jennings. Knowing he shouldn't, he pulled her closer, pleased by the way she felt in his arms. Trevor felt as if the thermostat in the Rose Room had been set ten degrees higher.

Unlike their other forms of communication, he and Claire danced in perfect rhythm. If they'd practiced for a month, they couldn't have given their guests a more impressive performance. Trevor found himself wishing the music would never end. When he and Claire didn't have to talk, or reason, or compromise—when they could just dance—they seemed made for each other.

The music crescendoed to a big finish. Well, he and Claire would show them. When the band played the last bars of the song, Trevor twirled Claire around, then leaned her back the way he'd seen it done in several old movies. The dated gesture suited tonight's audience.

Claire assumed the position gracefully and they finished just as the band did. The board members and their wives sprang to their feet and clapped their hearts out.

Trevor suddenly realized he was still holding Claire, although the music had stopped. He released her abruptly. The board members and their wives moved onto the dance floor and the band broke into a smooth rendition of "Moon River." Margaret Ward asked Trevor to dance at the same moment that Jacob Lawrence whisked Claire away.

Trevor stared at the plump, blue-haired lady in his

arms and suddenly missed Claire. But the radiant woman who smelled of jasmine had moved on.

That will be what happens eventually, he realized. When they figured a way out of this mess. Trevor would return to the apartment that he missed more with each passing day. Claire, too, would move on. Out of his life.

Trevor saw her dance by in her grandfather's arms and remembered how it had felt to hold her. Except for that dance, he and Claire had been out of synch ever since they met. They'd moved in perfect step for those brief moments and had given a remarkable performance for their guests.

It isn't only the dance that's a performance, Trevor reminded himself. Their entire relationship was a huge fabrication. Make-believe, with no more grounding in fact than a Grimm's fairy tale.

The song ended and Josephine Noble claimed the next dance. The first thing she did was step on his foot. The board members' wives made Trevor realize how truly magical those moments were when he'd danced with Claire.

People began moving back to their tables and Claire sank gratefully into her chair. She couldn't have danced and made small talk one more second. People chatted all around her. Trevor talked with Mrs. Noble and Granddad was laughing with one of his colleagues. Fortunately, no one quizzed her about her nonexistent marriage.

Tonight was the longest night of her life. The reception line had seemed to extend for miles. And when the waiters served dinner, Claire thought she couldn't choke down a single bite. If it hadn't been for that delicious punch the waiter brought that had miraculously soothed her stomach, she would never have survived. The waiter came by again and refilled her glass and she gratefully took a sip.

As troubled as Claire felt at interacting with all the members of the Brookshire Board, it hadn't proved the most disturbing part of the evening. That had come when she found herself alone with Trevor.

Claire could almost feel his hands on her back as he tried to dislodge her zipper. Trevor's nearness intoxicated her and she'd felt a great relief when he freed the zipper and she could put distance between them.

But not for long. In the car, he'd given her the beautiful corsage. And when he'd pinned it to her dress, she again felt trapped. Trevor spun a web of magic that she couldn't escape.

When they'd reached the country club, the only comforting aspect of the evening was that they were in a crowd. But then they danced and all the people in the Rose Room faded from existence. Claire adjusted her steps to Trevor's and they melded into one person. She would remember that dance as long as she lived.

When the song ended, Trevor didn't immediately let her go so the magic lasted a moment longer. Then he suddenly released her and the look in his eyes changed from tenderness and longing to the noncommittal expression she knew so well. A curtain had lowered and Claire felt suddenly cold. And lonely. Trevor changed, in the blink of an eye, from the gentle, yet passionate man into the authoritative Headmaster of Brookshire School.

Trevor leaned toward her. "I just saw Mrs. Noble yawn. That's a good sign. When she starts wearing down, these shindigs usually come to an end."

Claire suddenly felt so bone tired she didn't think she could walk out to the parking lot. Mrs. Noble came toward them. "I hope you young people have enjoyed yourselves."

"We loved the reception," Trevor said, sounding gallant again. "It was a great evening—one we'll never forget."

The understatement of the century, Claire thought. She turned to their hostess. "How can we thank you for all you've done?"

Josephine Noble patted her hand. "By having a wonderful marriage and a long, happy life together."

No chance of that, Claire thought, feeling an unexpected touch of sadness.

They said their good-byes and walked out to the Jag. "Well, we survived," Trevor said as they got in the car and pulled onto the highway.

"Just barely. I can't believe we have to do this all over again."

"Do it again? You mean there's another reception?"

"Not another reception. But the wedding shower's Tuesday evening. Torture of a slightly different sort."

"But I won't have to attend. Men don't go to showers," Trevor said matter-of-factly. He reached over and patted her hand. "I know it will be tough on you, Claire. I'll be thinking of you."

She chuckled. "You'll do more than think of me.

Cindy told me they've decided to make it a couples' shower."

She knew he'd stiffened, knew that his expression had turned stone cold. "Well, you'll have to tell Cindy that's impossible. Tell her I have a previous commitment."

"Not on your life. They've already sent out the invitations. And I'm not going through this alone."

They rode in silence until Trevor turned onto Mulberry Lane. As they walked up the sidewalk, he sighed. "Things just move from bad to worse."

Claire unlocked the front door and flipped on the light. When they stepped inside the entryway she turned to him. "We can still confess, Trevor. It won't be easy but we could do it."

He frowned and his brow furrowed. She thought about reaching out and stroking his forehead, trying to erase the frown lines that made him appear so solemn.

"I suppose we could. But we're too tired to make important decisions tonight. Let's sleep on it. Good night, Claire." He turned and headed for his room.

Claire stood in the dimly lit living room and unpinned the corsage. As she breathed in its sweet fragrance, she mentally reviewed the evening's romantic moments. Especially the dance and how marvelous it felt to be in Trevor's arms.

As she headed for her room, she almost wished this marriage wasn't a sham. That it wasn't a fantasy world she was living in, but a real world. A world she and Trevor could share.

But that would never happen and she knew it.

Chapter Six

Claire awoke feeling groggy after the torture of last night's wedding reception. She slipped into a sweatsuit and tried to force the nightmare event out of her thoughts. She'd lived through the ordeal and that was more than she'd expected. But she must get her life back on track, free herself from the conflicts that had plagued her since the first moment she met Trevor Mathison.

Meditation would help. Pulling the meditation mat she'd purchased in the Far East and her brass candlestick out of the hall closet, she went to the living room and placed the mat of woven straw in the center of the floor. She lit the taper and assumed the lotus position, centering her attention on the candle resting on the mat in front of her. She let the image of the flame burn into her consciousness and focused all her energy on its light.

One by one, Claire released her problems and let them

drift into space. She'd give them to the universe. See if the universe could figure out what to do with them since she couldn't. As the minutes slipped past, a deep peace permeated every cell of her being.

She sensed a healing begin—a healing from the upheaval of last night and all the chaos of recent days. As she approached the theta level of consciousness, the world seemed nebulous. Surreal. And gloriously peaceful.

"Claire?"

The deep voice barely penetrated her subconscious.

"Claire?"

It took several agonizing moments before she could pull out of her relaxed state.

"Claire, where are you?"

As Trevor's voice cut into the well-being that encircled her, she tried to force her body and mind back into the present. As she stood up, her foot bumped the candle and it tipped over, instantly igniting the straw mat.

"Oh, no! In the living room, Trevor! Quick!"

Trevor appeared from the hallway, wearing a blue velour robe and slippers, and looking sleepy. He glanced at her, then noticed that the mat was on fire. "What in the name of good sense . . ."

He raced over to the mat and lifted it by the edge that was not burning, shooting her a glance that was hotter than the flames. "Open the front door," he commanded, and Claire raced around him to do so.

The headmaster ran outdoors, the fiery mat in his hands, the belt of his robe trailing behind him. "Turn on the garden hose," he commanded and she hurried to the faucet and turned the water on hard. Trevor tossed the mat onto the grass and Claire aimed the hose at her mat that was only half its former size and shrinking fast. Unfortunately, the pressure had built up in the hose and the water spurted out unevenly and with great force. Claire hit Trevor in the back with the powerful spray and he let out a whoop as the cold water penetrated his bathrobe. "Not me," he yelled. "The mat!"

She finally hit her mat which was now only a remnant but at least the fire was out. Except for the belt on Trevor's bathrobe! Claire realized, panicking again. Flames raced up the narrow piece of fabric heading straight for the headmaster. The only thing Claire could think to do was turn the hose on him again. She soaked him good.

Trevor sputtered and flailed his arms. "What are you doing?" He escaped the spray, strode to her side, and snatched the hose from her hands.

"You were on fire," she said desperately.

"The mat was on fire," he said, his dark eyes crisp as charcoal.

"First the mat was on fire. Then it was you."

His eyes pierced to her very soul. "I would know if I was on fire. There would be heat and there would be pain."

Claire felt like a disobedient child who'd been sent to the principal's office. "Look at your belt, if you don't believe me."

He stared at the singed fabric and reluctantly accepted her story. "Couldn't you have just told me? I'm not a gasoline tank. I won't explode."

"I didn't want you to get hurt." Claire almost wished she'd let the flames heat him up a bit.

Trevor shook his head. "Let's go indoors before the neighbors start to gather." Grasping her arm, he ushered her into the house.

Once inside, Claire realized Trevor was a mess. The top of his robe was slightly damp, and from the waist down it was soaked. Water dripped down his legs into his brown leather slippers.

Claire felt a bit guilty. "Why don't you change clothes and I'll scramble us some eggs."

He frowned. "That would be too much trouble."

"I wouldn't suggest it if it was too much trouble."

"Okay, then. I'll be right back."

In the kitchen, Claire took a carton of eggs from the refrigerator and started whipping them vehemently to vent her frustration. The benefits of her meditation were long gone and stress had again reared its ugly head.

By the time she'd prepared the eggs, made toast, and got the coffee perking, Trevor returned. He wore stone-washed jeans and a plaid sport shirt and looked perfect again. "Good thing I came along to put out that fire," he bragged.

"If you hadn't come along, there wouldn't have been a fire," she snapped, tired of hearing him sing his praises.

He raised his eyebrows. "And why not?"

"I was meditating when you called me. When I heard your voice, it took a while for me to pull out of my meditative state. When I stood up, I accidentally bumped the candleholder. That's why there was a fire." She slammed two plates of eggs on the kitchen table.

For once, Trevor didn't have a comeback. They ate in silence and had just about finished when the doorbell rang.

Claire went to answer it. "Good morning, Mrs. Darling," she said, dreading a visit from her nosy neighbor. "Won't you come in?"

Mrs. Darling followed Claire into the living room and settled in the recliner. "While Frank was mowing, he saw a man come running out of your house carrying a fiery carpet," the woman declared. "Then, he saw you spray the man with your garden hose." Mrs. Darling was breathless as she repeated the incident. No doubt this was the most exciting neighborhood event she'd witnessed in years. "Did someone break into your house, Claire?"

"No, nothing like that." Claire almost wished there had been a robbery. It would have been less stressful. And easier to explain.

"I wanted to be sure you're all right. As you know, Claire, I don't meddle. I mind my own business. But it pays to keep your eyes open. I've certainly learned that."

"Thanks for checking, Mrs. Darling, but I assure you I'm just fine."

Mrs. Darling looked a little disappointed. "Well, who was that man? Do you know him?"

Claire had hoped her neighbor's curiosity could be satisfied without more information but it wasn't to be. "Yes, I know the man."

"Well, who is he?"

Claire sighed, preparing to launch into another telling of the lie. "The man is my husband."

Mrs. Darling's chubby fingers fluttered up to her cheeks. "Your husband?"

Now the whole neighborhood would know about their marriage. Mrs. Darling would spread the news faster than the fire that had consumed Claire's meditation mat.

"His name is Trevor Mathison," she explained. "He's Headmaster of the Brookshire School for Young Ladies."

Mrs. Darling rubbed her hands together as she absorbed the news. "Well, isn't that something. Looks like congratulations are in order."

"Thank you," Claire said lamely, wishing Mrs. Darling would just go home.

"Claire, sweetheart, could you hurry up?"

Trevor's deep voice rang out loud and strong and Mrs. Darling shot out of the recliner like a discharged bullet. "I must be going." She scurried to the front door.

"Come back again," Claire called, relieved to see Mrs. Darling retreating, but furious with Trevor for his sadistic little joke. She could add "a warped sense of humor" to Trevor's growing list of faults.

She headed for the kitchen where Trevor sat at the table, chuckling. "Why did you do that?"

He shook his head. "What a busybody. It sounded like you needed rescuing."

Trevor's knight-in-shining-armor complex had surfaced again. "Mrs. Darling is the biggest gossip in Fairfield. She'll spread the news of our marriage all over town."

Trevor sighed. "Might as well make it interesting. At least Mrs. Darling will have a nice day."

He carried his plate to the sink. "I've got to get away

for a while, Claire. I told my sister I'd come to Center-view this morning. The farm is the only place I can get a break from this insanity. At the farm things seem log-ical. Sensible. The way my life used to be before . . ."

"Before you met me."

"You took the words right out of my mouth."

"Well, that goes both ways. My life was a lot calmer before I met you." They glared at each other for several moments, caught in a deadlock.

She looked away first. "You're lucky you have family to visit. My only escape is meditation."

Trevor felt an inexplicable stab of compassion. Poor mixed-up Claire. Maybe she couldn't help it that she'd lost control of her life. Maybe she'd never gained control in the first place.

He couldn't believe his eyes this morning when he saw her in the living room with her straw mat shooting flames toward the ceiling. He never knew what to expect from Claire Jennings—only that it would be wild and wacky.

After he'd carried the mat outside to safety, Claire had hosed him down. Twice. But looking at her now, she didn't seem so wacky. She appeared genuinely miserable. "I suppose I could take you with me."

She sighed. "No thanks. All this pretending is driving me crazy."

The fleecy pink sweatsuit she wore made her appear soft and somehow vulnerable. For a moment, Trevor considered pulling her into his arms, holding her close, and telling her that things would be back to normal soon. But how could he? Normal was just a hazy memory.

"Angie knows the truth about us so you wouldn't have to pretend," Trevor said, knowing he should leave this alone.

She brightened. "That's right. It might help to get away for a while. If you're sure I won't be a problem."

A problem? Claire Jennings? Her comment sobered him—made him turn lose of his desire to protect her. Who would protect him from his pretend wife?

And now he'd invited her to the farm. If the farm was his only refuge from the craziness, why was he taking the craziness along? Would he ever learn?

After Claire changed into jeans and a red turtleneck, she and Trevor walked out to the Jag. The fall day felt unusually warm, a tribute to Indian summer. The sun shone bright and the clouds looked like mounded marshmallows.

Claire glanced at Trevor who looked totally in charge as he maneuvered the Jag over the country roads. They didn't talk much and the ride passed pleasantly. When they reached a road marked HH, they turned right, drove a mile further, then turned onto a gravel road that curved its way to a white frame farmhouse.

As they got out of the car, the screen door of the farmhouse banged shut and an attractive young woman with hair as black as Trevor's came out to meet them. She was shorter than Trevor but had similar features and the same snapping black eyes. "Hello, Trev." She came over to embrace him. "And you must be Claire. I'm Angie."

"Hi, Angie. I hope you don't mind my tagging along."

"I'm delighted you came. I just made some sun tea. Why don't we sit on the porch?"

Angie led the way to a cozy table covered with a blue and white checked tablecloth. As they took their places, she poured the tea. "How was the reception?"

"A nightmare," Claire said, and Trevor said, "Horrible" at the exact same moment.

Angie laughed. "Tell me all about it."

"I met the board members and their wives and they congratulated us on our marriage," Claire explained. "They served a wonderful dinner but my stomach felt so queasy I couldn't eat much."

"As usual, Mrs. Noble planned a dance," Trevor added. "It was one high-stress evening."

Angie passed Claire the sugar. "So the Brookshire Board is convinced you two are married."

Trevor nodded. "Completely convinced."

"What will you do now?"

"I thought you might have a suggestion," Trevor said. "I've given you a week to think about it. Claire and I are so busy getting school started, attending social events, and putting out fires that we haven't had time to find a way out of this marriage."

Claire ignored Trevor's crack about fires. He seemed less intense here at the farm. He looked more relaxed than she remembered seeing him—except for that fateful evening when he'd fallen asleep in her recliner.

Angie smiled. "So you actually want your big sister's advice."

Trevor glanced at Claire, humor sparkling in his dark eyes. "Some big sister. Angie arrived in this world just two minutes ahead of me. But she never lets me forget it."

Claire quirked an eyebrow. "You're twins?"

Angie nodded.

"No wonder you're so close." Claire felt a little envious at the bond Trevor and Angie shared. "I always wanted a sister."

"Are you an only child, Claire?"

"Yes. My parents were entertainers. They traveled a lot and left me with Granddad. He treated me great but I always thought life would be more fun if I had a sister."

"Is that the grandfather who heads the Brookshire Board?" Angie asked.

Claire nodded. "One and the same."

"The grandfather who gave you the ultimatum?"

Claire shot Trevor a disapproving glance, feeling suddenly betrayed. Had he blurted out her whole life history to his twin sister?

Angie picked up on Claire's irritation. "Don't be angry with Trevor. We tell each other everything. We're not only twins, we're also best friends."

Claire couldn't believe that the tough-minded Headmaster of Brookshire School had a gentle side. Or that this engaging, bright-eyed young woman was Trevor's sister and confidante. "Is there anything about me you don't already know?"

Angie smiled. "A lot. And I can tell just from meeting you that we're going to be friends."

Surprised by the honest, forthright comment, Claire said, "I'd like that."

"Why don't the three of us take a walk in the pasture.

It's such a gorgeous day. My husband Sid went to purchase a cow from a neighboring farm. When he gets back, we'll all go to the Truckstop Café for lunch."

Claire expected Trevor to resist, but he didn't, so they set out. He held up a strip of barbed wire for them to slip under and they ambled down a hill that led to the pond. The air smelled clean and fresh and butterflies darted all around them. A robin in a cottonwood tree sang its heart out. They didn't talk much, letting the beauty of the countryside speak for itself. When they reached the pond, Angie and Claire sat on the dock while Trevor skipped rocks over the smooth surface of the water.

Trevor, handsome as ever, gave his full attention to making the rocks hit the water, bounce into the air, then hit again and again. He seemed as exuberant as a child.

Angie chuckled. "Trev's trying to impress you."

"Well, he's succeeding. Rock-skipping is one skill I didn't know he had."

Angie reached out and touched Claire's arm. "Trevor has lots of talents, but he doesn't often let people close enough to see them. He seems relaxed around you, Claire."

She smiled at Angie, and didn't point out that Angie had it all wrong. Trevor Mathison did not feel the slightest bit comfortable in her presence. But he seemed different today. Claire liked this laid back side of him she hadn't known existed. And she already liked Angie who was the most open, gentle person she'd met in ages.

Trevor finished skipping rocks and walked toward them. When he sat beside Claire on the dock, his thigh touched hers and she had to fight off a sudden rush of pleasure at his nearness. His musky cologne mingled with the fresh scent of the outdoors. And for a moment, sitting close to Trevor and talking companionably with Angie seemed the most natural thing in the world.

"Come on, sis. You've been mulling this marriage thing over all week. What can we do to get out of this mess?"

Trevor's question cast a shadow over Claire's jubilant mood. For the moment, she'd forgotten about the foolishness that had turned her life into a soap opera. The sun slipped behind a cloud making the morning less bright.

Angie shook her head. "I've thought about it a lot, Trev, but I'm stumped. Maybe the simplest thing would be for you and Claire to get married. For real, I mean. That would solve all your problems."

Angie had gone too far, Claire realized. Trevor would be furious. "Getting married might be the simplest solution, but it would never work," Claire said before Trevor could reply. "We'd be divorced in a week."

"Divorce!" Trevor shouted the word as if it was a new concept to him. "That's it! We'll get a divorce!"

Claire had never seen anyone quite so elated about divorce. "How can we do that when we're not even married?"

Trevor ran a hand over his chin. "We'll tell the board our marriage isn't working out . . . that we've made a mistake. Then we can quietly 'divorce' and get on with our lives without losing credibility."

Angie shook her head. "Divorce won't solve your

problems, Trevor. The board wants a married man for their headmaster. You've told me so a hundred times."

"And a divorce would humiliate Granddad," Claire added. "We've never had a divorce in our family. Plenty of unhappy marriages, but never a divorce."

They sat in silence for several moments. Finally, Angie said, "Maybe we ought to continue this discussion on the walk back to the farmhouse. Sid's due back any time."

The return trip held none of the fascination with nature Claire had experienced earlier. And her sense of camaraderie in the company of Trevor and Angie had also disappeared. These two people weren't her family, after all. They were virtual strangers.

Sid waited for them on the front porch of the farmhouse. He seemed very nice and lunch passed pleasantly. By mid-afternoon, Claire and Trevor said their good-byes and headed back to Fairfield—back to the marriage that wasn't. Any joys the day had brought dissipated as the full awareness of their predicament again hit home.

"I guess you're pretty miserable in this pretend marriage," she told Trevor as they drove along. "You certainly got excited at the prospect of divorce."

"Isn't that what you want, too? Wouldn't you like it if I returned to my apartment tonight and you could get your house back?"

"Well, yes," she said, feeling just a little hesitant. In spite of all the trauma this situation caused, Claire wasn't quite sure she wanted Trevor to just pick up and go.

"Did you like Angie and Sid?" he asked.

"I sure did. You have one terrific sister."

"Yeah, I know. But she sure wasn't much help. Angie can usually cut through all the layers of a problem and zero in on a viable solution." He shook his head. "Not today. She disappointed me."

"You mean when she suggested we get married because it was the easiest way out?"

"Yeah. That was the dumbest thing Angie ever said."

His comment seemed harsh and Claire's discouragement intensified. While she didn't want to be tied to Trevor any more than he wanted to be tied to her, did he have to imply that marrying her was the stupidest idea on earth?

It was, of course. Two people must have things in common if they planned to spend the rest of their lives together. And she and Trevor were as different as two people could be. As far as she'd been able to determine, all they had in common was that they both worked at the Brookshire School.

It was a relief to get home. Claire needed time to herself. And some space. "Thanks for the nice day, Trevor. I really enjoyed it."

The telephone rang and Claire hurried into the living room to answer. After she finished the conversation, she turned to Trevor. "That was Cindy Lewis. She sounds excited about the shower."

Trevor shrugged. "I suppose someone ought to be. For us, it's just another endurance contest."

Claire felt suddenly overwhelmed. "I can't believe things have gotten so far out of hand. Marriage is supposed to be a sacred commitment between a man and a woman. Not the farce we've trumped up."

"I won't argue that point. Listen, I've got to run up to my office for a while. See you later."

After he left, Claire, wasn't as happy to be alone as she'd thought. She felt a little lonely. She'd enjoyed the time she'd spent with Trevor and his twin. For one crazy moment, she wished this marriage was real and that Angie was her sister-in-law.

If Trevor was more like Angie—reasonable, agreeable, nonjudgmental—maybe they could have built a relationship. They might have taken his sister's suggestion and turned the pretend marriage into a real one. But sadly, the only resemblance between Trevor and Angie was physical. If it weren't for the strong family likeness, Claire would not have believed these two were related. How could the relaxed Angie have the same blood coursing through her veins as strict, unbending Trevor Mathison?

She sighed. Trevor was more like Granddad than his own twin sister. That made Claire want to be particularly careful. As much as she loved her grandfather, he'd always tried to control her life.

And she certainly wouldn't marry a man with those same tendencies. She'd had enough male dominance to last a lifetime.

Chapter Seven

On Monday morning, the avalanche of girls tumbled back into Claire's classroom. The noise level seemed a few decibels lower than last week and Claire felt grateful for small favors. She rapped on her desk with a ruler. "Please take your seats, girls."

The chattering finally diminished. "We'll be studying Hawaii this week. What year did Hawaii become a state?"

No response. The girls weren't participating in class discussion the way Claire had hoped.

Suddenly Lee Ann Adams, the short redhead, raised her hand. The gesture surprised Claire since Lee Ann was the first girl to observe any kind of protocol.

"Yes, Lee Ann?"

The girl frowned. "I don't know the answer, Miss Jennings, but I'd like to ask a question of my own."

103

Creative thinking. That's what Claire hoped to foster in her students. "Go right ahead."

"My great-grandfather's on the Board of Directors for the Brookshire School. He told me that the board gave you and Mr. Mathison a wedding reception at the country club on Saturday night. Is that true?"

As snickering broke out in several parts of the classroom, Claire realized it was essential to keep her career and her private life separate. She frowned. "What does your question have to do with Hawaii?"

"Nothing. Unless you and the headmaster go there on your honeymoon." The snickering turned into laughter and all eyes focused on Claire.

Now what? If she shared a little of her personal life would it help her bond with her students? At least she had their attention. While they weren't enthralled with history, they seemed fascinated with her marriage.

She took a steadying breath and decided to relent. "I'll give you five minutes to ask personal questions. *Appropriate* personal questions. Then we'll get back to the lesson. And please raise your hands."

Hands waved like stalks of wheat on a windy day. Claire called on Suzanne first. "How long did you and Mr. Mathison date before you got married?"

Trouble already. They hadn't dated at all. "About six months," she said, crossing her fingers behind her back. "Next question."

"Is the headmaster romantic?" Allie Davidson, the platinum blond with the long curly hair, asked the question which stirred up more embarrassed giggles. Why had she agreed to this exercise in torture?

"Yes, he is romantic. On Saturday, Mr. Mathison gave me a lovely corsage. And he's an excellent dancer." She uncrossed her fingers. Those answers were actually true.

"That's cool!" said Tina. "Does he snore?"

More giggles.

"That's not an appropriate question." Claire was glad she'd added a qualifier because she had no idea whether Trevor Mathison snored or not. "Cindy?"

"Did you pick out a china pattern?"

"Not yet. But that's a good idea. We'll consider it."

Cindy beamed.

"Two more questions," Claire said matter-of-factly.

Hands waved vigorously as the girls leaned forward in their seats. Claire called on Amy Lang, suspected frog stasher. "Did you have a wedding shower?"

"The teachers are giving us one tomorrow evening."

Claire was glad she could answer another question honestly, although the thought of the shower distressed her to no end. "Last question."

Several hands still waved and she chose Sally Brown, a quiet, reserved girl. "Do you and the headmaster want to have children?"

The room fell silent and Claire considered ruling the question out of order. If anyone other than the pensive Sally had asked it, she probably would have. What could she say? She wanted children but she had no idea whether Trevor did or not. And even if he did have children, they wouldn't be hers. They'd belong to his wife, if he ever found one. Considering his overbearing personality, Claire thought that highly unlikely.

For a brief moment, she pictured what their children

might look like. A blue-eyed girl with long blond braids. A boy with shiny black hair and a cowlick like his father's.

"Miss Jennings?"

The "Miss Jennings" and the expectant look on Sally's face brought Claire out of her musing. "We haven't discussed a family yet. We want to get to know each other better first. All right, girls, back to work. Who can tell me when Hawaii became a state?"

No one could.

"Open your books to page thirty-five."

Groans. Lots of them. All the enthusiasm vanished as the girls dragged out their textbooks and began to study.

Thank goodness the quizzing was over. The question and answer session had been uncomfortable. But the girls' interest level was high. If she could get them as excited about history as they were about her private life, she'd be on her way to becoming a good teacher.

As the girls studied the chapter, Claire reviewed the science lesson she would teach after lunch. She glanced up from her reading to see Cindy Lewis beckoning to her. Claire went to the door.

"Several teachers have asked for gift ideas," Cindy whispered. "They said you aren't registered at any of the area stores. What should I tell them?"

Cindy seemed as excited about the shower as Claire's students had been while prying into her private life. She had to suggest something. "We could use some glasses," she said. "And some towels."

"Do you need sheets? What size bed do you and Trevor sleep in?"

Claire felt her cheeks flush. How bizarre that everyone else assumed . . . Her fellow teachers, her students, the neighbors, all thought she and Trevor were married. And now Cindy asked about sheets. "Qu-queen size," she stammered.

"Thanks, that helps. I'll let you get on with your preparation."

Back at her desk, Claire's mind started to wander. She recalled the fateful night that the headmaster moved in with her. She remembered how stern he'd looked standing on her front step—hanging clothes bag in one hand, briefcase in the other. And she'd been in for quite a surprise later that evening when she'd taken a snack to Trevor's room. Up until that moment the only thing she'd seen him wearing was a suit and a stiff white shirt.

When Claire saw Trevor stretched out on her bed, dressed in jeans and a T-shirt that showed off his strong upper body, she'd caught her breath. What a transformation! The man looked positively delectable. Claire was amazed to see the muscular physique hidden under all that starch.

Cindy's innocent question had sent Claire's thoughts back to that evening and her first realization that her "husband" was more than the outspoken headmaster of a respected girls' school. He was also a hunk!

Hawaii didn't hold the girls' attention and the noise level began to rise. Claire saw Lee Ann throw a paper wad with expert skill. It hit Kelly Freeman—the girl with the electrocuted hair—on the chin. Why Lee Ann wanted to tempt fate by picking on a girl twice her size was beyond Claire.

Kelly let out a startled shriek and shot Lee Ann a killer look. "Sneaker breath!" Kelly screamed.

Lee Ann went for Kelly with the speed and skill of an experienced street brawler. Other girls began taking sides, cheering them on.

"Stop it, girls. Stop it this minute!" Claire insisted, but she could hardly hear her own reprimand over all the racket.

The girls continued to scuffle and Claire had almost reached them when a powerful male voice cut through the commotion. "What seems to be the problem, Miss Jennings?"

The headmaster! At times Claire thought of him as Trevor. His sister even called him Trev. But at this moment there was only one thing to call him. The headmaster! He appeared out of nowhere as if he'd been airlifted from above. While he looked like a fashion model from *GQ,* he carried himself with the authority of a military policeman.

The girls immediately quieted. Several of them gazed at Trevor with dreamy expressions and the room became so quiet you could hear a pin drop.

"As I was walking down the hall, I heard an inordinate amount of noise coming from this classroom," he said.

Inordinate? Claire bet most of her students couldn't define or spell that word. *I'll put it on a spelling test,* she thought nervously, wondering how to resolve this latest crisis.

"Kelly and Lee Ann had a little misunderstanding, Mr. Mathison," she explained, glaring at the girls who had separated and stood panting but silent. "The situation is under control now." That should impress him. Control was his fetish.

"I certainly hope so. Take your seats immediately, girls," he said to Kelly and Lee Ann who seemed frozen in place. They walked stiffly to their desks and sat down. "May I speak to your class for a moment, Miss Jennings?"

She couldn't very well refuse. "Go right ahead, Mr. Mathison."

He walked to the front of the classroom and began pacing. "As sixth-graders, you girls are the most mature students at the Brookshire School," he said pensively. "The younger girls look up to you. They think you're special. But if they see you fighting, or hear a lot of noise from your classroom, they get the wrong idea. I'm sure you don't want that to happen. You want to set a good example, right?"

No one said a word. They would probably rather set fire to the building than set a good example.

Trevor leaned toward them, his dark eyes shining. "Right, girls?"

"Right," came the chorus.

He folded his hands and smiled. "That's better. Now, I'll be keeping an eye on you. Miss Jennings is a new teacher this year and she needs your cooperation. I'm sure you want to make her first year of teaching a good one."

Claire nearly laughed out loud. They'd rather burn her in effigy than make this year any easier.

"Kelly and Lee Ann, report to my office immediately,"

the headmaster ordered. "Brawling in the classroom is inexcusable."

Annoyance began to dominate Claire's thoughts. She couldn't let Trevor step in and take over. She was the authority here. "Mr. Mathison, I'm sure the girls have learned their lesson," she said crisply. "I will see to it that they understand their mistakes and don't repeat them."

The headmaster frowned. He hesitated a moment, then said, "Very well, Miss Jennings. They're all yours." He turned on his heel and left the room. His footsteps resounded crisply as he walked down the polished tile hallway.

As Trevor returned to his office, he felt both angry and disappointed. He'd been appalled by the amount of noise coming from Miss Jennings's classroom. It sounded more like a football game in progress than class in session. When he did step in, it only took a moment to see that Claire had lost control. Good thing he'd come along to help break up the fight. She obviously couldn't manage it herself.

The encounter confirmed Trevor's worst fear. Claire did not have what it took to keep the sixth-grade class in line. She granted entirely too much freedom. Not that this behavior was new for Kelly and Lee Ann. They'd battled their way through third, fourth, and fifth grades. He'd had them in his office plenty of times for scuffling on the playground or roughhousing in the halls. But they'd never fought in the classroom. Until today.

He'd better have a serious talk with Claire before she formed any more bad habits. He'd head for her house early tonight and have a heart-to-heart talk with her. He couldn't tolerate lackadaisical discipline. The school year was just beginning and the time to nip inappropriate behavior—both in the students and his teachers—was during first term.

His job as headmaster required that he keep things running smoothly and he intended to do just that. Claire Jennings would need to shape up—or leave Brookshire.

Trevor pulled the Jag into the driveway and lifted his briefcase out of the backseat. He strode to the front door and unlocked it. The house was quiet.

"Claire?"

"In the kitchen."

He found her at the table, drinking tea again.

"Can we talk?" He placed his briefcase beside the chair and sat down.

Claire's eyes caught his. "You bet we can."

She seemed angry. She'd probably had a tough day. If the few minutes he'd spent in her room were an indication of how her day had gone, she no doubt felt discouraged and exhausted. This little chat was well timed.

"I'd like to talk about what happened in your classroom today."

"Funny, I'd like to discuss that myself."

Claire's cheeks were as rosy as a sun-kissed peach. He had learned to tell that she was angry by her skin color. He remembered the blotches on Claire's neck the night of their "wedding reception." "Having the girls fight in class today probably upset you," he said, trying to show understanding.

"The girls didn't upset me," she said crisply. "But your entrance into my classroom did."

"What are you talking about?"

She glared at him. "I have to make my own way with my students. I'm their teacher and they must learn to respect me and follow my instructions. When you stormed in this morning, you usurped my authority."

"Usurped your authority?" he asked incredulously. "The only people with any authority in your classroom this morning were Kelly and Lee Ann. If anyone staged a coup, they did. Why are you mad at me?"

"You came at a bad time," Claire defended, and he tried to ignore the fact that she was especially pretty when angry. Her blue eyes blazed gloriously. "The morning went quite well up until that moment. And the afternoon was terrific. You happened to walk by at the one time when things were, shall I say, difficult."

"Of course, things went smoother in the afternoon," Trevor said, feeling frustrated with her for failing to understand the problem. "I laid down the law." He sighed. "Claire, I told you when I hired you that students need a firm hand. Especially this class. If you don't take charge, they will."

Her magnificent eyes continued to blaze. "But you have to give me a chance, Trevor. It takes time for the girls to respect me and to know what the limits are. You set me back by barging in like a bull elephant. You made it harder for me, not easier."

"A bull elephant? Wouldn't you call that an exaggeration?"

She crossed her arms and her lips formed a pout. "Just slightly."

She'll never get it, Trevor thought, feeling annoyed at how badly this little talk had backfired. He'd better ease off for now. He'd made it clear what he would and wouldn't tolerate and Claire Jennings would have to live by his rules whether she liked them or not.

"We're both tired," he snapped. "Let's finish this discussion some other time."

"Fine with me."

Trevor stood and went to his room. He took off his suit and tie and pulled on sweatpants and a T-shirt. One thing was perfectly clear. He and Claire Jennings would never find common ground. Certainly not at school. Their teaching philosophies occupied opposite ends of the spectrum.

And their "marriage" was another disaster. The outside world seemed pleased about it but he certainly wasn't. He missed his privacy and his apartment more and more. And Claire seemed as miserable as he.

What a mess! What a colossal, mixed-up mess he and Claire had created by being unwilling to confess the truth to Jacob Lawrence.

Claire immersed herself in lesson plans, trying to forget the unpleasant conversation with Trevor. Their problems seemed to increase with each passing day. Trevor didn't approve of her. She knew she fell short of every expectation the man ever had. And his expectations were legitimate where her teaching was concerned. Claire didn't see how she could ever please him.

To be perfectly frank, she wasn't delighted with him as a principal. He'd barged into her classroom to once again save the day. Claire knew she wouldn't handle every problem perfectly, but she'd learn ... right along with the girls. If the headmaster would give her a chance.

A nagging thought tugged at Claire: Could she have regained control of the situation by herself? Had she overreacted to Trevor's intervention? She had to admit that the girls were pretty far out of hand. She'd probably never know the answer to that question. But if she wanted to keep her job, she'd have to stay in the headmaster's good graces. She probably should declare a truce. But how?

An idea flashed into her thoughts. When she'd stopped at the market after school to buy fruit, she'd impulsively picked up a box of chocolate doughnuts. She thought it only fair to have a few snacks around the house that Trevor enjoyed, even if they did send his cholesterol soaring. His soaring cholesterol was the least of her worries.

She'd make a peace offering. While their "marriage" didn't stand a chance, this job had to work out. In the beginning, Granddad had been Claire's chief motivation. But there was more to it now. As the days passed—even the really hectic ones—Claire realized that she loved teaching. She wanted to succeed at teaching more than anything in the world.

She heaped doughnuts on a plate, poured two tall glasses of milk, and arranged the refreshments on a tray.

She carried it into the living room, placed it on the coffee table, then went to Trevor's room and knocked. "I thought you might like a snack," she told him.

He opened the door a crack and his scowl deepened when he saw her. "Thanks, but I can't face any more vegetables today. I had two for lunch: one green and one yellow. That's enough for anybody."

He started to close the door but she put her foot in it. "The snack isn't vegetables. Why don't you come to the living room and see?"

He followed her out, reluctance written all over his face. But when he spotted the heaping tray, his eyes brimmed with pleasure. "Chocolate doughnuts. My favorite." He helped himself to several and sat down on the couch.

Claire took a doughnut to be sociable and sat beside him. After they'd munched a while in silence, she said, "I'd like to ask you a favor, Trevor."

"Oh? What's that?"

"Be patient with me for a while. I want to be a good teacher, but it takes time to build rapport with students. I know we don't see eye-to-eye on discipline, and I realize that you have more experience. But I have reasons for my methods. I don't want the girls to behave because they're afraid. I want them to develop good moral judgment and practice self-control."

Trevor listened patiently. "I know it's tough to get school started, and being a first-year teacher makes things doubly difficult. I just want you to get off to a good start, Claire. By the way, these doughnuts are delicious."

He appeared more interested in the snack than in philosophizing about discipline. Realizing she'd better enjoy this uncharacteristic response, Claire sat back and nibbled on a second doughnut while Trevor finished his third and went for a fourth.

He glanced at her and the casual look in his dark eyes made her heart skip a beat. "Maybe we both need a break from school and the pressures of our fake marriage. What if we declare a moratorium and go out to dinner tomorrow evening?"

Her own eyes widened in disbelief. "You mean together?"

He chuckled. "Of course, I mean together."

Is he asking me for a date? Claire wondered. But the words "date" and "moratorium" canceled each other out.

She suddenly remembered and felt a sinking feeling in the pit of her stomach. "We can't go out tomorrow night. It's Tuesday."

He looked baffled. "Don't you eat dinner on Tuesdays?"

"Of course, I eat dinner on Tuesdays. But we have other plans. Tomorrow's the wedding shower."

Trevor stopped mid-bite. "Oh, yeah. I forgot."

He looked stressed, too, Claire realized. His circumstances weren't easy either. Not at school or at home. And this wasn't even his home. "When's the last time you've been back to your apartment?"

"Funny you should ask. I stopped by this afternoon. The place looked good." He sighed. "I sure miss it."

"What's your apartment like, Trevor?"

"It has three bedrooms and a spacious living area with

a vaulted ceiling. Plus a large dining room and a good-sized kitchen."

"What kind of furniture?"

"Contemporary. I don't have a lot of furniture but what I have I've selected carefully. I like clean lines. An organized look."

If she pictured the absolute opposite of her place, Claire could probably imagine Trevor's. She saw peace in his eyes as he talked about his apartment. It must be as hard for him to live here as it was for her to have him.

The events of the day and the taxing demands of their circumstances suddenly seemed overwhelming. Trevor was miserable and so was she. This ridiculous charade was destroying both their lives.

She sighed deeply. "What can we do? This arrangement is killing us."

Trevor set his glass of milk on the coffee table and turned toward her. "Maybe we should quit fighting it. Take Angie's suggestion."

"You mean get married? For real?"

"It's the only thing we haven't tried. Maybe we ought to stop resisting fate."

Claire shook her head. "We both deserve better than that. When you marry, it needs to be to someone you love with all your heart and soul. Someone who excites you and sends your pulse racing. You've got to feel the fireworks." She shook her head again. "A platonic marriage is the worst possible solution."

Funny, her own pulse had quickened as she spoke. She glanced at Trevor, who sat close to her on the couch, and his powerful magnetism again seemed to overwhelm her. The man might be tough and he might have ideas on discipline she'd never subscribe to, but she couldn't ignore his overt masculinity. His cologne reached out to her as if it were a physical presence. And he looked incredibly handsome in sweat pants and a T-shirt.

Claire wanted to stroke his cheek that showed just a hint of beard and ruffle the cowlick that had shot up again. She welcomed that one stray shock of hair because it made him look vulnerable—made him more of a regular guy than the controlling headmaster.

But regular guy didn't define Trevor. Superhunk was more accurate. Everywhere he went, women noticed Trevor. She'd have to be blind not to realize that females of all ages were attracted by his charm and good looks. The board members' wives had done everything but drool over him at their reception. And her students were equally impressed. They'd shaped up fast when Trevor Mathison entered the room.

"I found someone like that once," he said, and Claire had to think hard to remember what they'd been talking about.

"I was engaged to a girl who made me feel the fireworks," Trevor continued. "Jessica and I were very different but we loved each other deeply. At least I thought we did. My whole world revolved around Jess." He paused, obviously hesitant to continue.

"What happened?" Claire asked gently.

"While I was making wedding plans, Jess ran off with my best friend." His laugh was harsh. "All she left me was a note."

"I'm so sorry, Trevor."

He shrugged. "I don't look for fireworks anymore. Two people have to be a lot alike for a marriage to work."

Horrors! Claire thought. She couldn't imagine a woman with the same rigidity as Trevor Mathison. The two of them would produce little robot children who would someday rule the world.

"I don't agree with you. I believe opposites attract."

He shook his head. "They attract, all right, but that's not enough. Look at Jess and me." He gazed straight ahead and seemed lost in his thoughts. Finally, he said, "You remind me of her. Jess loved life and approached everything with enthusiasm. But the relationship couldn't last. We were too different."

As Trevor remembered Jessica and the strong chemistry that had sizzled between them, he felt the same desire and deep yearnings stirring inside him for Claire Jennings. Tonight she'd pulled back her platinum hair with a black ribbon and wisps of it had escaped, curling softly around her face. Claire looked especially alluring. Even the difficulties of the day hadn't significantly dimmed her bright spirit.

Knowing he shouldn't, Trevor reached out and tucked a wisp of hair behind her ear. She drew in a quick breath but he didn't let that stop him. He reached for another strand of hair that curled gracefully at her shoulder, and caressed it between his fingers. It felt like cornsilk.

Claire's pretty mouth beckoned to him with the power of a giant magnet. He leaned toward her, wondering how those lips would taste. As he continued to lean closer, he fully expected Claire to stop him. Desperately hoped she would stop him because he couldn't stop himself.

But she didn't. And when his lips met Claire's, her soft mouth yielded to his more demanding one and he lost himself in the power of the kiss. He pulled her closer, delighting in her sweetness and in the feel of her mouth on his.

For several moments, they were lost in a world entirely their own. All thoughts of the Brookshire School vanished as did the many complications of their pretend marriage. The pleasure it gave Trevor to kiss Claire far surpassed his wildest imaginings.

Instead of rejecting his embrace as he'd expected, Claire slipped her arms around him and continued the kiss. Was she as magnetized as he?

Trevor's fingers touched the black satin ribbon that held her hair in place and he untied it. Her long hair tumbled around her shoulders, spilling over his hand, emitting a powerful allure all its own. He threaded his fingers through the silky strands and got lost in the wonder of her.

Claire's heart pounded in a dangerously fast, erratic fashion. When Trevor had first leaned toward her, the movement caught her off guard and she hadn't turned away as she knew she should. And once his lips touched hers, the magic of his mouth held her. She felt as unable to resist as a fly caught in a silky spiderweb.

Lost was the only way she could describe herself. She felt captured in the addictive wonder of her pretend husband's kiss. Her senses reeled and swirled and when Trevor deepened the kiss, her resistance weakened further.

She had to stop this insanity, but her heart wasn't co-operating. It wasn't on her side anymore. It was drowning in the sweet taste of Trevor's slightly-chocolate kiss.

After an eternity of feeling lost, she finally mustered up the courage to pull away from him. It took every ounce of strength she had and was harder than coming out of the theta level of consciousness. But she must still the torrents of emotion that stripped her of all reason.

The sound of a bell cut into the quiet and for a moment Claire couldn't tell if it was the telephone, the doorbell, or just a noise inside her head. Fortunately, Trevor seemed more in touch. "I'll get it," he said huskily. He walked to the door while Claire sat cemented to the couch, experiencing the waves of aftershock Trevor's kiss had set in motion.

"Good evening, Mr. Mathison. I'm Sadie Darling."

Claire heard her neighbor's high-pitched voice echo in the entryway. "I've brought a wedding gift to welcome you to the neighborhood."

"How kind," Trevor said politely. "Won't you come in?"

How can Trevor sound so calm and in charge of himself? Claire wondered. She guessed this was one time that being a control freak came in handy.

"I'll only stay a minute," Mrs. Darling said. "But I would like to see Claire open the gift."

"Claire? Mrs. Darling brought us a present." Trevor's voice was calm and stable. He sounded for all the world like a docile, caring husband.

Claire finger-combed her hair into place, remembering that only moments earlier, Trevor had run his fingers through it. His touch had filled her with roller-coaster emotions that refused to die down.

"Please sit down, Mrs. Darling," she offered. "May I get you some coffee?"

"Why, that would be lovely."

Mrs. Darling sat and as Claire walked to the kitchen, her legs felt weak from her most recent encounter with Trevor. She took several deep breaths, trying to get her body and mind to function as a team again. But she felt strangely out of touch—far removed from the present moment. She steadied one hand with the other as she poured the coffee. Returning to the living room, she passed a cup and saucer to Mrs. Darling who was updating Trevor on the latest neighborhood gossip.

"Would you care for a doughnut?" Trevor offered, and Mrs. Darling helped herself.

"This is our first wedding gift," Claire said, feeling the need to make conversation. At least she could tell the truth again. It was a rare privilege these days.

Mrs. Darling smiled. "Several of the neighbors went together."

The gift, carefully wrapped in pink foil paper, sported a huge silver bow. Claire tore into the package, her fingers still shaking. Was that caused by the after-effects of Trevor's kiss? Or because she was opening a gift she wasn't entitled to? She sighed, realizing she'd better keep a record of all the presents so she could send them back when this charade ended.

Claire lifted the box lid. "It's an electric blanket," Mrs. Darling announced. "Queen size."

Claire coughed nervously as she lifted the light blue blanket from its box. "How lovely."

"It has dual controls," Mrs. Darling explained, pleased as punch about the revelation. "That way you can both be comfortable." Mrs. Darling fidgeted uncomfortably.

"Thank you for being so thoughtful." Trevor's voice boomed out of the fog that had surrounded Claire since the moment his lips had touched hers.

Mrs. Darling recovered her composure. "You don't have to be afraid to sleep under the blanket, because it has radiation protection. We thought it was a practical gift. Something every married couple can use."

Maybe every married couple could use a dual control electric blanket but what on earth would she and Trevor do with it, Claire wondered? Cut it in half? She imagined you could shock yourself pretty badly doing something like that.

"Thanks for the gift," Claire said, suddenly feeling punchy. The day had been overloaded with stressors. First the quizzing by her students, then the brawl between Lee Ann and Kelly which was followed by the headmaster storming into her classroom. If that wasn't enough, Trevor's nerve-jangling kiss and the arrival of their first wedding gift capped the evening.

As Trevor escorted Mrs. Darling to the door, Claire realized that his intrusion into her classroom hadn't affected her nearly as intensely as his intrusion into her heart. One kiss had changed everything.

Another frightening revelation teased her thoughts. She'd just discovered that where Trevor was concerned, she couldn't trust her heart. It had a mind of its own.

Her heart had deserted her and sided with the enemy without so much as a backward glance.

This couldn't go on. She had to get Trevor Mathison out of her house and out of her life. And the sooner the better.

Chapter Eight

On Tuesday afternoon, Claire left school as soon as the last bell rang. As she headed across the Brookshire campus, the September sun warmed her and a gentle breeze ruffled her skirt.

Leaves were turning rich colors, leaving behind the monochromatic green of summer. Clusters of rust and gold chrysanthemums dotted the hillsides. A perfect autumn afternoon like this normally brought Claire great pleasure. But not today.

Tonight's wedding shower loomed ahead like a prison sentence. How could she face another counterfeit evening? At times like this, she wanted just one thing: to confess and reclaim her life.

She drove slower than usual, hesitant to face what lay ahead. As she approached her subdivision, she was surprised to see Trevor's car in the driveway. What was he doing here? He never came home till after supper, and usually not till bedtime.

As Claire opened the front door, she heard hammering coming from the basement. She tossed her books on the small entryway table and went downstairs where she found Trevor nailing boards together. "What are you making?"

He glanced up at her, five nails protruding from his mouth, and perspiration dripping from his forehead. He wore a white T-shirt that was soaked from his labor and clung to his body like a second skin. He also wore a pair of torn denim jeans that she was surprised he even owned. Sweat, nails, and torn denim jeans. Not the head-master's usual image. Claire felt like she was looking at one those drawings in a children's book that asks: *What's wrong with this picture?*

"I'm building shelves," he answered, his speech muffled by the nails. "To help you get organized."

So this, too, was about organization. "What do you want me to put on these shelves?"

"Wedding presents. For now, anyway. After we return the gifts, you can use the shelves for your teaching materials."

"That's a good idea."

Trevor wiped his forehead with his handkerchief and pulled the shelf he'd just constructed into place alongside two other perfect wooden structures. "I took the afternoon off to build them. Say, would you hold these nails a minute?"

Claire obliged and with a single, fluid movement Trevor pulled the damp T-shirt over his head and tossed it onto his toolbox.

Claire had known Trevor would have a muscular chest judging from the terrific arms she'd discovered the night he'd moved into her spare bedroom. But the real thing extended beyond her musings. She inhaled deeply, not wanting to let Trevor know that the sight of his chest turned her knees to jelly.

He reached for the nails and his fingers brushed her palm, causing prickly sensations in her arm. "I don't suppose you have time to help me?"

Claire felt a need to escape from her own basement—to break free from the powerful hold Trevor had on her emotions. Maybe it would help to open the basement windows and get some air circulating. She glanced at the windows which were open wide. "I have a few minutes," she said, feeling obligated to help. But she prayed for a cold north wind so Trevor would put his shirt back on.

"Just steady this board."

And who will steady me? Claire wondered as she held the board in place.

Trevor started pounding. That helped a little. The force of the hammering compelled Claire to pay attention to the task. If she didn't hold tight, the board would go flying across the room. The exertion helped her regain her composure.

All the racket helped, too. It resounded in her ears and between the deafening noise and having to hold the board steady, Claire could stay in the same room with this Adonis.

She did have to close her eyes once or twice to lessen

the impact of his rippling muscles as they expanded and contracted with the labor. Even that didn't help much. She'd already seen him, and his powerful physique was permanently branded into her consciousness. Trevor's woodsy cologne and warm masculine scent—mingled with the smell of sawdust—attacked her senses, making matters even worse.

He finally finished and set the fourth shelf beside its three counterparts. Claire heaved a relieved sigh, grateful beyond belief that she'd completed the difficult assignment. She took a step back to examine his handiwork. Of course, the shelves were perfect. She imagined Trevor's children would be very much like these shelves. Flawless. Proud. Impeccable. "They're wonderful," she declared. "And they'll be very helpful."

"I'm glad you approve," he said, and Claire wondered if he'd read her mind and realized it wasn't only the shelves she approved of.

"Now I'd better get cleaned up," he said. "I've got some paperwork to do before we go to the . . . the . . ."

He couldn't seem to bring himself to say the word. It must be paralyzing him with fear the same way it was paralyzing her. "The shower," she finished, and he nodded.

He started collecting his tools and reached for a broom to sweep up the sawdust. "I'll do that," Claire offered.

Trevor smiled. "Thanks for your help, Claire." He took the stairs two at a time and disappeared.

Claire grabbed the broom and began sweeping vigorously, trying to regain her equilibrium. She'd just seen another surprising side of Trevor. She knew he could do great things with his mind, but didn't know he could work so well with his hands.

She swept the sawdust into a dustpan. The fresh smell of the new wood mingled with the scent of Trevor's woodsy cologne that stayed behind to taunt her.

Claire dumped the sawdust into the trash barrel, then went to brew some tea. At least she had time to regroup. She kicked off her shoes and took the tea to her recliner and sat down.

She hurriedly finished her tea. She set the cup on the end table without checking what the tea leaves had to say. It was probably more bad news and she had all she could manage.

She couldn't stay here. She must get away. She scrawled a quick note for Trevor in case he wondered where she'd disappeared to. "Went for a walk," it said. "Be back in time for the shower."

Cindy Lewis lived in a tiny house. Minuscule, actually. As Claire watched the teachers and their spouses pouring in, she wondered if Cindy would start hanging people from the ceiling or stuffing them into her closets.

"I know my house is small," Cindy apologized, "but I didn't want to have the shower at school. It's too impersonal."

Finally, all the people arrived, packing the little house to overflow. A mountain of gifts heaped in one corner of the room cut the floor space significantly. People sat on Cindy's overstuffed furniture, on the folding chairs Cindy had placed in two short rows in her dining area, and on pillows on the floor.

Cindy herself sat cross-legged on the last available spot: her coffee table. She raised her hand for silence and the conversation stopped. "I want to thank all of you for coming tonight to support our headmaster and his bride."

Oh, no. More clapping. Jack Johnson's elbow punched Claire repeatedly in the ribs as he clapped in enthusiastic support.

"I think we'll have the newlyweds open their gifts first, then Trevor can load them into his car and that will give us all a little more room," Cindy suggested and everyone cheered.

"Now remember, Claire," Cindy cautioned, "each ribbon you break represents the birth of a baby."

Claire felt her face flush. "We're not ready for children so I'll be very careful."

"Trevor, if you'll open the cards and read them, I'll keep a list of your gifts," Cindy told him.

"Good idea." Trevor handed Claire the first package. "You do the honors, honey." He slit open the envelope. "This one's from Betty and Jack Johnson."

Trevor's use of the word "honey" sent an unexpected thrill zipping through Claire. She tore off the wrapping and lifted the lid. "Drinking glasses. How nice."

At least glasses were neutral. If they didn't receive any suggestive gifts, Claire just might survive this painful ordeal. She lifted one cobalt-blue glass and admired it. "Thanks, Betty and Jack."

Claire broke the ribbon on the next package and sighed inwardly. "There's your first baby," Cindy said triumphantly.

Trevor didn't find that amusing. "We'd better get to know each other first."

Claire wholeheartedly agreed. If their guests had any idea how little she and Trevor knew each other, they'd be appalled.

The gifts came at Claire as fast and furious as her students poured into the classroom. A lace tablecloth. A tea kettle. A steam iron. At least all the gifts were neutral.

"Aren't there ever any guy gifts at showers?" Doug asked. "Like hammers, screwdrivers, socket wrenches?"

"Hang on a minute." Coach Smith dug through the pile of presents and handed Trevor an oblong package. "Try this."

Trevor opened it. "A soldering gun. Hey, thanks."

"I kept the receipt in case you already have one," Coach volunteered.

"I don't. This is great. Thanks."

Next came two casserole dishes. Then Trevor handed Claire a large box. "It's from Cindy and Doug Lewis."

Claire removed the wrapping, careful not to break another bow. She removed the lid and lifted out a lacquered box with elaborate carving on top. "It's gorgeous." She smoothed her fingers over the glossy surface and glanced at Trevor who seemed as pleased as she.

"Trevor gave me the idea," Cindy said. "When I asked him what you especially liked, he suggested something Asian. Your husband knows you pretty well, Claire."

Tears teased the back of Claire's eyes and she had to blink rapidly to discourage them. Having Trevor suggest such a personal gift was yet another surprise. "I love the chest. I'll keep it in a special place in my . . . in our home."

Trevor reached over and squeezed Claire's hand, and for one magical moment, everything seemed real. Claire felt like Cinderella at the ball and allowed herself to bask in the glory of the occasion. Being surrounded by generous, supportive friends made the fantasy almost believable.

She broke the ribbon on the next box, dissipating the dreamy mood. "That's baby number two," Cindy announced and Claire felt her cheeks flush at the prospect.

She again pictured a neat, disciplined little boy who held the hand of his blond-haired, blue-eyed sister. As those images teased Claire's thoughts, she wondered what kind of father Trevor would make. Probably loving and dedicated.

Claire's daydreaming ended abruptly when she opened the package and discovered queen-size sheets. Sheets could not be classified as neutral! This present packed a double whammy!

The navy and green plaid linens came from Trevor's secretary, Diane Ridings. "These match the electric blanket we received last night," Trevor announced, giving Claire a sideways glance.

Claire bit her tongue to keep from snickering as the whole scenario with Mrs. Darling and the dual-control, radiation-protection blanket flashed into her thoughts. By biting hard, and not looking at Trevor, she stifled the urge to giggle.

Finally, they reached the last gift. "It's from all us girls," Cindy said, handing it to Claire. "You fellas better close your eyes for this one. Everyone but the groom, that is."

Now what? Claire wondered as she slowly pulled off the tape. The pure, white paper looked too perfect, too chaste to tear. Besides, Claire dreaded seeing what the box contained.

The room grew quiet. Like typical males, the fellows' eyes were glued on her, waiting to discover what the box contained that they weren't supposed to see. Claire lifted the lid and parted the tissue which revealed a gown as pure and chaste as the wrapping paper. Translucent— bordering dangerously on transparent. And for one ridiculous moment she pictured herself modeling the gown for Trevor.

"Hold it up, Claire," one of the guys teased. "We've seen stuff like that before."

Claire felt her cheeks flush. By now, she probably had stage-three blotches all over her chest. But this time she'd outsmarted the blotches by wearing a high-necked blouse. She lifted out the gown that was edged with elegant lace. Tiny white satin rosebuds lined its plunging neckline. Claire held up the filmy creation and tried to hide behind it all at the same time.

Doug Lewis nodded his approval. "Not half bad."

Coach Smith slapped Trevor on the knee. "I don't know about you, but I call that a guy thing."

"Every bride needs one really special gown. We hope you like it, Claire," Cindy said.

"I absolutely love it." Claire meant every word.

Thankfully, things started moving after the presents were opened. Some of the women helped box the gifts and Trevor stood to stretch which immediately cut Claire's stress level in half. He carried boxes to the Jag, assisted by Doug and Jack, and Claire felt freed. But she couldn't think about that now. She had more evening to live through.

After Trevor loaded the last of the boxes into the Jag, he let the pleasant evening air cool him. Doug and Jack had gone back inside and Trevor sat down on Cindy's porch steps, desperate for a break. The days were growing shorter. He glanced at the sky complete with a bright moon and fanfare of stars and breathed deeply. The worst of the evening was probably over. At least all the gifts had been opened.

This wasn't his first wedding shower. Jessica's large family had thrown one for them just two weeks before Jessica left him. While Trevor hadn't been invited to that shower—it was ladies only—they'd insisted he stop by afterward for refreshments.

Jessica seemed happy that night. She'd shown him each of their gifts and appeared genuinely excited. There had been no hint of the impending breakup. That's why the note she left him hit with the impact of a Mack truck.

Tonight's shower stirred up all those distressing memories. Trevor remembered the excitement he'd felt about marrying Jessica and how that had been dashed by her betrayal of him. Claire reminded him so much of his former fiancée. She had the same carefree spirit. And like Jess, Claire was incredibly beautiful.

Staying at Claire's was getting more and more difficult because his physical attraction to her grew stronger each day. Trevor sighed, wondering how much longer he could play act his way through this comedy of errors. He must find a way out, and soon. He stood and stared into the dark sky, wondering how to escape from this make-believe marriage.

"Trevor?"

Claire's soft voice broke into his thoughts. She pushed open the screen door and came out onto the porch. "Cindy wants us to cut the cake."

He sighed again. "Might as well play this out to a big finish." He opened the door for Claire and they walked down the narrow hallway to Cindy's tiny kitchen.

Trevor had to hand it to his teachers. They hadn't missed a trick. A huge cake with creamy white icing and peach-colored roses took up most of Cindy's kitchen table. TREVOR AND CLAIRE was inscribed on the cake with flowing letters. And underneath their names, the words: A FOREVER LOVE.

He almost laughed out loud. A forever love wasn't part of his future. Jessica hadn't even made it to the altar. He would never put himself through that agony again. Giving yourself to another person, being totally vulnerable, opened the door to debilitating pain. He'd certainly learned that the hard way.

Cindy handed him a knife. "Now cut two pieces of cake and then you can feed each other."

Who dreamed up all these goofy traditions? Trevor wondered. Claire's neck looked kind of blotchy. This must be stressing her, too.

Together they cut the cake and Claire held a piece so he could take a bite. As he steadied her hand, he noticed that her skin felt soft as rose petals. Then he held a piece for her, and took a long, hard look as he stuffed her pretty mouth with cake.

Claire Jennings was a knockout. He bet every man in the room envied him. His heart skipped a beat and his palms felt suddenly damp.

He'd kissed those enticing lips last night, just before Mrs. Darling showed up with the high tech electric blanket. And for a little while, all the craziness in Trevor's head had cleared. For those moments that his lips claimed Claire's, he could actually imagine them as a couple. She'd slipped her arms around him and pulled him close, making everything seem incredibly real.

"Kiss your bride, Mathison," one of the guys shouted.

"Go for it," another chimed.

He did. A platonic peck . . . nothing like last night's intense kiss. But it affected him in much the same way. It made him want more of Claire Jennings. Much more.

"You call that a kiss?" the Coach sneered. "Surely you can do better than that."

Trevor felt his manhood being challenged. He pulled Claire close and covered her pretty mouth with his own. All the fireworks that had exploded inside him last night returned for an encore. And Claire didn't respond passively. Just like last night, she kissed him back.

For a moment Trevor forgot anyone else was in the room. He and Claire seemed lost in a world of their own. When Trevor heard the guys cheering, he remembered he was in Cindy Lewis's tiny kitchen. He released Claire and she gasped, catching her breath.

Coach nodded his approval. "Much better."

Cindy cut the cake for the guests and Trevor tried to

convince himself that he'd only kissed Claire because it was expected. The guys insisted and he'd been suckered into it. But he was just kidding himself.

After the refreshments were served, the evening wound down quickly. Since it was a school night, people started leaving.

When all the guests departed, Trevor and Claire thanked their hostesses, then headed for Mulberry Lane and started unloading boxes. "We might as well take these right downstairs," Trevor said. Claire nodded and together they carried their ill-gotten booty to the basement.

"I think we should shelve the gifts by category," Trevor announced. "You know, kitchen stuff on one shelf, bedroom stuff on another."

Claire flinched when he said "bedroom stuff" and Trevor realized how tired she looked. "Must we do this tonight?" she asked. "We're both pretty drained."

"I suppose not, but if we organize it now, we won't have to face it tomorrow."

She sighed and nodded, then started putting the glasses and teapot on the top shelf.

"I thought we'd label the shelves alphabetically. Bedroom stuff on the first shelf, kitchen stuff down further."

"How will we know how many shelves to leave free for bedroom items?" Claire asked, irritably. "Mrs. Darling could be out collecting funds right now. She might show up with bedroom furniture first thing tomorrow morning."

Trevor stiffened. "If you'd rather not shelve these tonight we'll do it later. But there's a reason to arrange things alphabetically. Then I can cross-reference the computer printout. I'll organize one list by names and another by gift items. That way we won't lose track of anything."

Claire wanted to take off running. She wanted to dash up the stairs, fling open the front door, and disappear into the darkness.

Maybe she'd head for the country. Go see Angie. If she could just discuss all this nonsense with someone as sensible as Trevor's twin sister, maybe some of the pressure would subside.

Trevor had turned obsessive again. She'd known the first night he'd moved in—when he wanted a schedule to shower by—that his left-brained behavior would push her over the edge. But as she looked at the perfect shelves he'd constructed, and the three-by-five cards he was taping to them right now, categorizing their plunder, she never dreamed the extent to which he would carry his organization.

As she watched him place the queen size sheets on the top shelf, right beside the electric blanket, Trevor reminded her of Grandfather Lawrence more than ever. Trevor *was* Granddad—in a younger, more muscular body.

She couldn't let herself fall in love with this man. The last thing she needed was a controlling husband.

The phone rang and Claire dashed upstairs to answer it. She wasn't terribly surprised when she heard Granddad's voice boom over the line. If anyone would approve of Trevor's shelving project, Granddad certainly would.

"How's my girl?" he asked. "Is that husband of yours treating you well? If not, he'll have to answer to me."

As usual, Granddad didn't leave any time for Claire to answer his questions. But that was just as well. This way she didn't have to tell any more lies.

"Claire, I want to take you and Trevor out to dinner on Friday evening," Granddad declared. "I've been giving a lot of thought to your wedding gift. I finally made the purchase and I'll give it to you when we go out."

Another present. Claire wondered which shelf Trevor would file this one on. "That's very thoughtful, Granddad. Let me check to be sure Trevor's free. I'll call you right back."

She went downstairs where her pretend husband continued working. He'd divided the *kitchen* category into subcategories: *dishes, glasses, cookware, utensils, and tableware.* Was there no end to this man's obsession with detail?

"Granddad called," she told him.

Trevor turned his attention away from the teapot he'd just placed on the *cookware* shelf, and frowned. "What did he want?"

"He wants to take us to dinner Friday night. So he can give us our wedding gift."

Trevor looked stunned. After a moment's hesitation, he said, "I may have to build another shelf."

Claire laughed. She couldn't help herself. She kept laughing until tears streamed down her cheeks. Trevor looked at her with a puzzled expression and then a smile teased his sexy mouth. "You're right. It is pretty ridiculous. All of it."

Claire wiped the tears from her eyes and took a steadying breath. "Maybe if we laugh once in a while, we'll hang onto a portion of our sanity. What shall I tell Granddad?"

"You'd better tell him that we'll go."

Claire went upstairs and dialed her grandfather's number. "Friday will be fine," she told him. "Trevor and I are looking forward to it."

"Good, good. I'll pick you up at six. That's quite a fellow you snagged for yourself, Claire."

Of course Granddad liked Trevor. Trevor was his clone.

"See you on Friday," she said.

After she hung up, Claire curled up on the sofa. She'd handled all she could for one night. She couldn't go back downstairs and pigeonhole any more wedding presents. Let Trevor file away. Categorize his heart out. He enjoyed that more than anything in the world.

While the laughter had refreshed Claire, the seriousness of their situation came back to haunt her. They'd dealt with all their challenges reasonably well—the reception, the shower, the masquerade they had to keep up at Brookshire each day.

But Claire couldn't even imagine dinner with Granddad. She'd felt trapped sitting between Jack Johnson and Trevor on Cindy's sofa this evening. That was nothing compared to what Friday night would bring.

Granddad and Trevor together. How would she hold up to the two of them? When she heard Trevor coming upstairs, Claire hurried to her bedroom and closed the door. She couldn't think anymore, certainly not in the organizational fashion that Trevor required. He'd dissected their shower and inventoried their wedding gifts as impartially as a clerk in a discount store.

Claire felt a deep sadness set in. For a short time tonight, the evening had contained a kind of magic. For several glorious moments, she let herself dream that she really was Mrs. Trevor Mathison. And that she and the headmaster were building a life together. But that was foolish. It would only make things harder when the time came for them to separate.

She couldn't afford to get sentimental. She must remain as objective as Trevor. That, she realized, was a mighty tall order.

Chapter Nine

Claire stopped by the teachers' lounge to check her messages and pulled out a memo from Trevor. It said:

All 4th, 5th, and 6th grade teachers may select two students from their classes to serve as conflict mediators. These volunteers will teach other students how to solve problems peacefully. Write the names of your class representatives on this form and return it to my office immediately. Conflict mediators will meet in the theater after school on Monday for training.

Mr. Mathison, Headmaster

When Claire reached her classroom, most of the girls had returned from lunch and several sat quietly at their desks. The girls' behavior had improved considerably.

"Headmaster Mathison has asked me to choose two girls from our class to serve as conflict mediators," she told them. "These students will help other Brookshire girls learn to solve problems without a fight."

At the word "fight" Lee Ann glared at Kelly and Kelly glared right back.

Claire ignored them. "Representatives from all classes will meet and learn about conflict mediation. I have two girls in mind for this appointment. Kelly and Lee Ann."

Amy gasped. "Miss Jennings, aren't you afraid they'll kill each other before the first meeting?"

Claire ignored the laughter rippling through her classroom. "I wouldn't have asked them to represent us if I didn't think they'd do a good job."

Kelly looked shellshocked and Lee Ann deathly pale. Claire encouraged them to go to the back of the room and discuss this possibility. At first, they just glared at each other but finally started talking. Ten minutes later, Claire went to check on them. "Have you reached a decision?"

Lee Ann shrugged. "I will if she will."

"I can if she can," Kelly affirmed.

"Good. I'll write your names on the form. You may return to your seats."

"May I have your attention, class?" Thirty heads looked up from their textbooks. "Many of you will accept class responsibility this year. Today is Kelly and Lee Ann's turn, but next time it may be yours. For us to become a strong class, we must support each other. That's why I'm asking for a vote of confidence. Put your heads down while we vote so you won't be influenced by anyone around you."

The girls lowered their heads and no one so much as wiggled. "All those willing to support Lee Ann and Kelly as conflict mediators, raise your hands."

Crossing her fingers, Claire waited for the results. Five hands raised slowly, then six, then ten. Eventually, hands shot up in all parts of the classroom.

"You may sit up," Claire instructed when they finished voting. The girls did so and studied her expectantly. "I'm proud of our class," she said, smiling. "The vote to support Kelly and Lee Ann was unanimous."

"All right!" said Angela. Amy started clapping and the rest joined in.

"Amy, will you take this form to the headmaster's office?" Claire asked. She'd considered sending her new conflict mediators but thought that was pushing her luck.

When Amy returned from the errand, she handed Claire a note from the headmaster. "Please report to my office after school today. We need to talk."

The taste of victory quickly subsided. While the note didn't mention a problem, Claire felt certain one existed. She could sense Trevor's displeasure in the perfect upper case letters he'd neatly printed on the page.

While she didn't like to think of it, Trevor had only issued her a four-week contract and two of those weeks had already passed. The only way to get a full-time position was to meet his rigid expectations. That seemed impossible.

What if Trevor terminated her after only four weeks of teaching? How would Granddad react to that bit of news? He'd have enough difficulty accepting the fact that she and Trevor weren't really married.

After school, she made her way to the principal's office and found Trevor gazing out the long, low windows that provided a great view of the campus. When he saw her, his brow furrowed slightly. "Come in, Claire. Sit down."

She did and Trevor closed his door. "I'll get to the point." He looked into her eyes and the intensity of his gaze drilled into her very soul. "Your choices for conflict mediators appalled me. How could you choose the two most difficult girls at the Brookshire School?"

Claire felt like a punching bag that had just taken a left hook. "I think Kelly and Lee Ann can do a good job."

"Based on what? Past experience? For three years these girls have been at each other's throats. One wrong look sets them off."

Claire folded her hands and fought to stay calm. "I know the girls have a problem. But by helping others deal with their anger, Kelly and Lee Ann can manage their own."

Trevor shook his head. "The fight-fire-with-fire approach won't work. Conflict mediators are our level-headed students . . . those others turn to when they lose control."

As Claire listened to his little speech, she felt her irritation mount. "I understand the job description, Trevor. You made that perfectly clear in your memo. But I believe in my representatives. They can handle it."

He sank into his desk chair and covered his face with

his hands. "You just don't get it, Claire. Letting Kelly and Lee Ann serve as conflict mediators would be a joke. The students will never take them seriously. Since no one knows about your choices, just submit two other names."

"Everyone in my class knows," she snapped, beginning to get thoroughly annoyed.

He leveled her an angry gaze. "These are teacher-appointed positions. Why does your whole class know?"

"Because I told them. We talk about everything."

"Then tell them you've changed your mind."

"I can't do that. Going back on my decision will destroy all the groundwork I've laid."

He sighed. "I should have let the classes vote on student mediators. Your girls have lived with Kelly and Lee Ann's feuds for years. They would never vote them in."

"That's where you're wrong. I asked for a confidence vote and it was unanimous."

Now Trevor looked baffled as well as frustrated. Claire stood and straightened her shoulders. "I've chosen my representatives. If you can't live with my decision, then you tell Kelly and Lee Ann they aren't fit to serve. Because I won't." She turned and stormed out of his office.

Trevor watched Claire go and sighed deeply. She just wasn't cutting it as a Brookshire teacher. Things got worse every day. And living with Claire was even tougher than having her teach in his school.

Her tiny, overcrowded house made him crazy, especially the spare bedroom where he slept. He'd crammed his clothes into the tiny closet with her out-of-season things and every morning he had to steam press wrinkles out of something or other. One morning it was his suit pants; the next, his dress shirt. Ever since he'd moved to Mulberry Lane he looked sort of rumpled and smudgy. He didn't know how much longer he could peacefully coexist with Claire in the state of cluttered confusion that she called home.

Maybe she doesn't know any better. That thought caught him off guard.

An idea teased at his thoughts. Maybe if Claire saw another way of doing things—a better way—she'd want to live differently. Maybe. Just maybe.

He worked until 4:30, then headed for Mulberry Lane. As he entered the house, he called for Claire.

"I'm in the living room."

He found her on the floor, surrounded by textbooks. Her briefcase was tossed on the recliner, her purse flung on the coffee table, its contents spilling out in an unruly heap because she hadn't zipped it. The couch was covered with papers to be graded. The room looked like a library that had been hit by a twister. And Claire—rosy-cheeked and pretty as a princess—sat in the middle of the mess.

Wrinkles disturbed the alabaster skin of her forehead. "Do you want to discuss my conflict mediators?"

"Not right now."

"Good. Care to sit down?"

He did, but there was no available chair. "I'll join you on the floor," he said, lowering himself between his pretend wife and the towers of textbooks. He sighed. "We're very different, aren't we, Claire?"

"I suppose so." She focused those lovely eyes on him, which caused him to momentarily lose his train of thought. He could drown in the swimming-pool blue of Claire's eyes.

"Trevor?"

He realized he'd been silent too long.

"You were saying that we're very different."

"Oh, yeah," he said, grateful to her for jump-starting his brain. "I just realized that I know you better than you know me. I've spent lots of time in your home," *such as it is,* he thought, "and you haven't even seen mine. Why not come over for dinner tonight?"

She looked hesitant.

"I want to show you my apartment . . . the way I live. How about it?"

She sighed. "Okay. I'll come."

"Good. Here's my address and directions. How's six-thirty?"

"Fine." Claire couldn't believe he'd drawn her a map. The man only lived a few blocks from here.

After he left, Claire closed her books. She felt strangely excited about Trevor's invitation. Did this qualify as a date?

She went to her bedroom and ruffled through the closet, hunting for something special to wear. Nothing caught her fancy. She searched for her pale pink dress with the scalloped white collar but couldn't find it anywhere.

It must be in Trevor's closet. She went to check the side of his closet that held her things and finally found the dress scrunched between a sweat suit and a pair of tan corduroy pants. She'd press it and it would do nicely.

She glanced at Trevor's half of the closet. Four suits hung with precision on their hangers. They looked perfect, almost as if Trevor were still in them. His clothing appeared as disciplined as the headmaster himself. And beside the suits hung a dozen shirts, organized by sleeve length and graded by color. The closet was a painful illustration of just how different they really were.

Claire took one of his shirts from the closet. An ivory button-down oxford. It smelled like Trevor. Impulsively, she buried her face in the crisp fabric, and for a moment felt him as close as when he'd kissed her. Realizing she was embracing a bodiless shirt, Claire returned it to its appointed spot, leaving the proper amount of space between this shirt and the surrounding garments.

After ironing her dress, she decided to wear her hair up and swirled it gracefully on her head. She slipped into the dress, then put on large silver hoop earrings and high heels. As she examined her reflection in the mirror, she wondered if Trevor would approve.

Half an hour later, she pulled into the driveway of the Mansion Apartments, feeling almost as nervous about seeing Trevor's apartment as she'd felt at her job interview. He answered the door, dressed in a textured ivory sweater and taupe corduroy slacks, looking more like a golf pro than a headmaster. "Hi, Claire. Come in."

As she entered Trevor's spacious living room, Claire caught her breath. The room was white. Pure white. White walls, white woodwork, white bookshelves, and the cushiest winter-white carpet her feet ever had the pleasure of treading on. She felt as if she'd stumbled into the heart of a blizzard.

He led her to a contemporary sofa that blended rich shades of plum and navy blue. "Have a seat," he said and she did, thankful that the sofa wasn't white, too. If it was, no one would ever find it in this room.

Trevor sat across from her in a stately, high-backed chair of forest green velvet that looked like it had been custom made just for him. "What do you think of my apartment?"

She glanced around, taking in the tasteful paintings that hung in perfect symmetry. Brass accessories were strategically placed on marble tables and on the mantel of a white fireplace.

Trevor was waiting. "Well?"

"It's, um, immaculate."

He raised an eyebrow.

"And very tasteful. It reminds me a little of an . . ." *Oh, dear, art gallery is all that springs to mind.* But she didn't think that would please him. ". . . of some of the places I visited in England."

He smiled, obviously pleased. "Dinner's almost ready. Come right this way."

Claire followed him through the living room into a kitchen that was also very white and very clean. The room could double as an operating room if the local hospital ever had a power failure.

Trevor picked up two stemmed dishes of shrimp cocktail and carried them to a long glass table in the adjacent dining room. Then he came back and prepared two plates of food. When he finished, the plates held sizzling steaks, baked potatoes, and French-cut green beans. When everything was ready, he pulled a chair out for her. "Do you like shrimp cocktail?"

"Very much." As Claire speared a shrimp with the tiny fork he'd provided, she prayed it wouldn't slip off the fork and put a smear of cocktail sauce on his white rug. After eating the last shrimp, she breathed a relieved sigh. As they cut into their steaks, she asked, "This really is your house, isn't it, Trevor? It's not a movie set that you've brought me to see? Or a model home?"

The sound of his laughter bounced off the vaulted ceiling. "Why do you ask that?"

"Because it's so perfect. And so beautifully furnished. Who's your decorator?"

"I do my own decorating."

Claire took another bite of steak. "This afternoon when you said we were very different, I had no idea how different. Coming to your apartment proves the point."

She's getting it, Trevor thought happily. What a brainstorm he'd had by inviting Claire here.

She looked lovely tonight. He couldn't stop admiring the lovely way she'd styled her hair. Her delicate jasmine scent drifted across the table toward him making him lightheaded. And the way the soft fabric of the dress clung to her accelerated his heart rate. He felt so sidetracked by Claire's good looks that he nearly forgot his reason for inviting her to visit.

When they finished dinner, she insisted on helping clean up and as they worked together in the kitchen, Trevor realized he liked having Claire in his home. They finished and went to sit in the living room and Claire seemed unusually fidgety. "I hope you enjoyed your steak."

"I did. Very much." She crossed one long, shapely leg over the other and smiled at him. It wasn't her relaxed smile, rather a polite version.

"Claire, are you uncomfortable here?"

"A little."

"I want you to enjoy yourself. What can I do to make you feel at home?"

"Mess something up." A trace of her real smile peeked through.

Trevor glanced around the room and for the first time it looked too neat even to him. Had he caught Claire's clutter disease? Impulsively, he picked up a throw pillow and tossed it onto the carpet. Claire chuckled and tossed down another one. With a swoop of his arm, Trevor cleared the magazines off the table. They fluttered to the floor and landed in a messy heap.

Her laughter filled the room, bringing it suddenly to life. Claire seemed relaxed for the first time all evening.

"Oh, thank you, Trevor. I couldn't stand all this perfection much longer. You know, it's a miracle that we've lived together this long without killing each other."

"I suppose it is."

She sighed. "You must miss your home very much."

"I do. I really need to get my life back on track. I know this hasn't been easy for you, either, Claire. I've invaded your space."

She glanced around his living room. "Now that I've seen your apartment, I understand how difficult it must be for you to live in my crowded little house."

"Maybe we should confess to your grandfather on Friday evening and bring this crazy business to a close."

She nodded grimly. "Let's give it serious thought."

"You've got a deal."

"I'd better go. I've got papers to grade."

As Claire picked up her purse from beside the sofa, her eyes suddenly brightened. "Trevor, why don't you sleep here tonight? If anyone drops by my house, I'll make up some excuse. I'm getting good at that."

The thought of staying at his apartment both pleased and troubled Trevor. While it provided a welcome refuge, he felt a tinge of regret at separating from his pretend wife. "Good idea," he said, pushing the absurd feeling aside.

She smiled. "Thanks for the wonderful dinner."

"My pleasure."

The evening air felt pleasantly cool as Trevor walked Claire to her car. Cicadas filled the night with their mesmerizing sounds and the moon was a slice of silver in the nighttime sky. It reminded Trevor of Claire's shiny hoop earrings. He took her arm and thought seriously about kissing her good night. Wanted to badly. But she didn't give him a chance. Instead, she slipped into her car and drove off into the darkness.

Trevor went back inside but his apartment seemed lifeless without Claire. And he hadn't accomplished his mission, either. His plan to teach Claire order and organization—by example—backfired. She'd been happiest when pillows and magazines littered the floor.

He sank into his high-backed chair. Opposites might attract, but they could also drive each other crazy. He'd learned that painful lesson when he fell in love with Jessica. So why didn't he squelch his growing feelings for Claire? He'd never be stupid enough to make the same mistake twice, would he?

The truth suddenly hit him. He hadn't been able to change Jessica and he'd never change Claire, either.

If he was smart, he'd quit trying.

Chapter Ten

Claire went to the spare bedroom and knocked. "Are you ready, Trevor? Granddad will be here in ten minutes."

The door creaked open. "The cleaners put so much starch in my shirt that I can't fasten the collar buttons."

"Here, let me help." She grasped one tiny button and tried to force it through its appointed buttonhole. "You're right about the starch. This shirt is stiff as a board."

He turned his head to give her better access and as Claire leaned closer, the seductive scent of his musky cologne made her tipsy. The fragrance, coupled with Trevor's powerful masculinity, nearly overwhelmed her, so she held her breath. She'd outsmart the sneaky substance that sent her emotions reeling.

Continuing to struggle, she forced the buttons through

their holes, then stepped back into neutral territory. "Dere. I fidaly got id buddoned."

"Thanks a lot. Do you have a cold?"

"Doe. I mean no," she answered, allowing herself the distinct pleasure of breathing again.

He walked to the mirror to knot his tie and she watched him manipulate the narrow piece of fabric until it hung perfectly in place. Then he turned to face her . . . a stunning male specimen, immaculately groomed and breathtakingly handsome. "What's wrong, Claire?"

She shrugged. "Nothing really. Guess I'm just a little nervous."

"Have you given any more thought to telling your grandfather the truth?"

The doorbell cut into their conversation and Claire hurried to admit Granddad—another perfect male specimen. Older and more distinguished, with gray feathering his dark hair, Granddad looked as well turned out as Trevor. Claire leaned to kiss his cheek and noticed that his cologne was different from the headmaster's. More spicy.

"I made six-forty-five reservations at the Terrace Room. Are you kids ready?"

"Almost. I'll get Trevor."

Claire returned to the spare bedroom and found her pretend husband staring out the window. "Granddad's here."

When Trevor turned to look at her, she saw despair written all over his countenance. "We've got to confess. I can't keep up this pretense any longer."

"Let's wait for the right moment. After Granddad has

a glass of wine, he'll be more receptive. And more forgiving."

"Sounds good."

As Claire walked out to Granddad's car, Trevor on one side of her, Granddad on the other, she felt like a prisoner on death row being escorted to her last meal.

It very well could be her last meal with these two men. If she and Trevor told Granddad they weren't married, Trevor would move out of her house—and Granddad, out of her life.

They settled into the front seat of Granddad's big Lincoln. As Claire sat sandwiched between the two powerful men, their combined scents mingled into an aromatic hodgepodge, making her feel slightly intoxicated.

"I hope you're both hungry," Granddad declared.

Trevor nodded. "I certainly am. It's nice of you to invite us to dinner, Mr. Lawrence."

"Mr. Lawrence sounds so formal. Call me Granddad."

"Granddad it is." The word "Granddad" kind of squeaked out of Trevor's throat, cracking his usual take-charge image.

Once inside the restaurant, they approached the maitre d'. "Right this way, Mr. Lawrence." The man ushered them to an elegant table topped by a crisp linen cloth, fresh flowers, and a lighted candle.

"How's Claire doing in her first few weeks of teaching?" Granddad asked as they took their seats.

Trevor hesitated. "Well, she's making progress. She has an interesting way of interacting with the students."

Claire sighed. Interesting way of interacting, indeed.

"And what's it like to have your husband as your

boss?" Granddad was actually waiting for answers to-night. Claire wished he'd ramble on as usual so she and Trevor wouldn't have to lie so profusely.

She sighed. "It's a lot to get used to. Trevor and I have opposing ideas about discipline."

"Hmm. Is that right, son?"

Trevor nodded. "I think teachers should rule with a firm hand—anticipate trouble and head it off. But Claire wants the girls to have more freedom of expression."

"And you think that's wrong?"

"Not wrong, exactly. But it's easier to keep control in the first place than to try and get it back."

Granddad nodded. "Well, those are both viable teach-ing styles. I'd say the Brookshire students are lucky to have a headmaster and a sixth-grade teacher who both care so much about them, even though your approaches do differ."

The open-minded comment surprised Claire. Maybe there was room for both their teaching philosophies at Brookshire School.

"You know, Trevor," Granddad said after they placed their order, "your wedding is the biggest thing that's hap-pened in our family since Claire's grandmother and I eloped."

Because Granddad seemed at ease, Claire let her guard down a bit. Trevor must have relaxed, too, because he suddenly reached over and took Claire's hand. The shock of his warm, strong touch sent a million megawatt surge of delight arcing through her body.

Granddad smiled. "It's great seeing you kids so much in love. That's how Sara and I felt from the moment we met. We had very different personalities, but that didn't stand in the way of our feelings for each other. During the day, I had a corporation to run, but the best part of my day was coming home to Sara. She'd have dinner waiting and soft music playing. You know, Trevor, those were the best years of my life." He sighed. "Sara died when Claire was four years old and life's never been the same since."

"You must have loved her very much." Trevor squeezed Claire's hand, reactivating the power surge. His hand felt strong and supportive. And oh so comforting.

Claire had braced herself for an evening of rigid conversation and authoritative comments. Instead, Granddad had turned sentimental. And Trevor was acting like a bridegroom!

When the waiter brought their steaks, Granddad said, "I told Claire on the phone that I finally purchased your wedding gift."

A troubled expression replaced Trevor's look of relaxed ease.

"I almost bought you kids a desk," Granddad continued. "A walnut roll top desk you could use in your study when you move to a bigger house. But I wasn't sure where you'd put it in the meantime."

Trevor looked relieved. "We don't have a place for something that large."

That's for sure, Claire thought. It would bust Trevor's shelves all to pieces.

"I finally decided there was nothing romantic about a compartmentalized piece of furniture." He slipped an envelope from his pocket and passed it to her. "I hope this will help you build memories."

Claire's hand shook as she accepted the envelope. She opened it and pulled out a colorful brochure that showed lovely Hawaiian girls in grass skirts dancing the hula on a sandy beach. EXPERIENCE THE WONDERS OF WAIKIKI, the pamphlet declared in bold type.

Claire took a deep breath, trying to calm her ragged nerves. "Oh, my."

"I've arranged with the board for you kids to take a week off in October so you can have a real honeymoon."

"Granddad, you shouldn't have," Claire said, feeling suddenly guilty about deceiving the generous man who had been her stabilizing force through her childhood years.

Trevor looked as startled as he had the morning Claire's meditation mat caught fire. "It's much too extravagant, sir."

"Nonsense. You kids should start your marriage with a little excitement."

Claire didn't think she could handle much more excitement. The Hawaii trip was the latest in a long string of shockers. The surprises rolled in as fast and furious as tidal waves. She and Trevor hardly had time to recover from one shock before the next one hit home.

She glanced at Trevor who seemed ready to tell the whole truth. But confessing felt all wrong now. If they were going to admit their guilt, they should have done so before Granddad gave them the gift. If they spoke up now, he would feel foolish. Like he'd been manipulated.

"Granddad," Trevor said, and judging from his obvious discomfort, Claire felt sure he was about to come clean. So she kicked him soundly under the table.

Trevor jumped and shot her an inquiring glance.

"What is it, son?"

Trevor looked back and forth from Granddad to Claire. "There's something you should know, sir."

Claire kicked him again. Harder this time.

"Speak up, boy. What is it?"

Trevor swallowed hard. "You should know, um, how much Claire and I appreciate this gift."

Claire released the breath she'd been holding. Thank goodness Trevor hadn't blurted out the truth just yet.

"Well, you kids certainly deserve it. I'm proud of your success as a teacher, Claire. And Trevor, you're the best headmaster Brookshire has seen in decades. But more important, you two make a terrific couple."

The beginning of a migraine teased Claire's temples and she longed to bring this evening to a close. They finally finished dinner and the waiter brought the check. "Would you mind dropping by my house on the way home?" Granddad asked.

While Claire didn't see how she could manage any more pretending, how could she refuse her generous grandfather?

"We'd be glad to," Trevor said, probably anxious for another chance to tell their sordid story.

They left the restaurant and drove to Granddad's where he ushered them into the library. "Have a seat, kids."

Claire and Trevor sat next to each other on the couch and Granddad settled in his favorite black leather chair beside the fireplace. As Claire looked at Granddad, she realized again how much he and Trevor were alike. Their manner, their carriage, their egos, even their favorite chairs. If Trevor's high-backed forest green chair were here, the two men could sit on either side of Granddad's fireplace like a couple of distinguished bookends.

Granddad leaned back and crossed his legs. The grandfather clock ticked methodically as Claire waited for the next bomb to drop. "The board discussed some pretty interesting matters at our meeting this week. One item will be of particular interest to you."

Trevor leaned forward. "Oh? What's that?"

Granddad folded his hands. "Several years ago the board considered building a house on the campus for our headmaster. We even had plans drawn up but shelved them because of finances. Our endowment recently increased and we're reconsidering building the house."

Claire's headache picked up momentum as Granddad served up the latest dose of stress. Trevor now looked pale and drawn. What happened to the relaxed man who'd held her hand earlier this evening?

Granddad went to his desk and spread out the architect's drawings. "Come take a look."

As Trevor studied the sketches of the colonial house with its stately pillars and long, curving driveway, he couldn't suppress his pleasure. He'd never dreamed the board might build him a house. His career was definitely on fast-forward.

Trevor tried not to see himself living in this amazing structure but he couldn't help himself. He could picture the Jag moving up the curved driveway to the attached garages. He could see himself striding up the wide stairway onto the porch after a long day at school. And, for an instant, he could imagine Claire in the house waiting for him—the way Sara had waited for Granddad.

Granddad pulled out another drawing. "Here's a sketch of the inside."

Trevor couldn't curb his mounting fascination. "What an incredible floor plan."

"And you'll love the kitchen, Claire," Granddad added. "Oak cabinets. Built-ins. The best of everything."

As Claire leaned over the sketch, her silky blond hair tumbled over her shoulders. The black-and-white dress she wore hugged her in all the right places, making Trevor painfully aware of just how beautiful Claire was. She'd be a wife any man would be proud of.

For a moment, Trevor wished the world they'd created wasn't a fantasy. If he and Claire were really married, this incredible house would be theirs.

"What do you think of the kitchen, honey?" Granddad inquired.

"It's magnificent."

Claire suddenly sighed.

"What's the matter, sweetie?" Granddad asked. "Too much excitement for one evening?" He reached over and slipped his arm around her and pulled her close.

She sighed. "It's a little overwhelming."

"Come on, then. I'll take you kids home."

They all piled back into the Lincoln. When they reached Mulberry Lane, they said their thanks and Claire unlocked the door and switched on a light. "Would you like a cup of hot chocolate, Trevor?"

"Thanks, I would."

He followed her into the kitchen and when the beverages were prepared, they took them into the living room and sat on the couch. "Most couples would be delighted with a honeymoon in Hawaii," Trevor declared.

"We're not most couples."

"That's for sure."

"I was afraid you were going to tell Granddad the truth at dinner."

He sighed. "That was the plan, wasn't it?"

"Yes. But the timing was off."

"So you kicked me under the table," Trevor declared. "Twice. I considered stopping by the emergency room on the way home. For stitches."

The smile that lit Claire's blue eyes warmed Trevor's heart. She'd looked particularly glum since Granddad pulled out the drawings for the headmaster's house.

"I know we decided to confess but we should have done it sooner. He would have felt foolish."

"You're probably right. Your grandfather's a great guy, Claire."

"Yeah, I know." She set her mug on the coffee table, tucked one leg under the other, and leaned back against the sofa cushions. "What did you think of those house plans?"

"Amazing. Simply amazing. A dream home, for the right couple."

Claire sighed and studied him with concern. "I'm really sorry about this mess, Trevor. It's all my fault. My poor memory started all our trouble."

"Your memory? You're blaming our problems on your memory?"

"Of course," she said, and he noticed that her hair was the color of the sand on the Hawaii brochure. "I forgot my briefcase and that's what set off this whole ridiculous chain of events." She proceeded to enumerate everything that had happened as a result of forgetting her briefcase.

Her monologue made Trevor chuckle. "If we told all that to your grandfather, he'd never believe it anyway. You just convinced me that when we do break up, we don't dare tell the truth. We'd better lie our way out of it."

She sighed. "We're getting good at that. Every morning I check my nose in the mirror. It's grown half an inch."

Trevor welcomed the flash of mischief that sparkled in Claire's lovely eyes. He reached out to touch the delicate nose that hadn't grown a single millimeter. Then he stroked her cheek.

He'd tried all evening to repress the image of honeymooning in Hawaii with Claire but it kept resurfacing. He could picture them swimming in the ocean, sunning on Waikiki, and dancing the night away. Forcing those tempting images from his thoughts, he said, "If nothing else, you've taught me to laugh at myself. You've shown me life doesn't have to be so serious and structured. That schedules don't rule the world."

Her pretty mouth curved into a smile. "Have I?"

Claire's lips attracted him like a seductive magnet. He leaned toward her and covered them with his own, hungrily exploring the sweetness of her mouth, drowning in jasmine, and the magic that was Claire.

She inched closer. When Trevor felt her softness against him, his senses began to swirl. He deepened the kiss, passion stirring every cell of his being.

When she finally broke the kiss and buried her face in his shoulder, he threaded his fingers through her silky hair and caressed the soft skin of her neck. He tilted her chin upward and traced her eyebrows, her nose, then her mouth.

"Trevor." His name burst from somewhere deep inside her and longing filled her voice. "Don't stop," she whispered against his neck. But he couldn't kiss Claire any more than he already had. He had been an honorable man—until the night he'd fallen asleep in her recliner. Since that event, he'd been living a lie. It had to stop.

Pulling out of Claire's embrace and forcing himself to stand was the hardest thing he had ever done. But he couldn't take advantage of her any longer.

"What's wrong, Trevor?"

Her throaty whisper threatened to destroy him. "Everything. We can't let this charade continue a moment longer."

She sighed but said nothing.

"I'll move out tonight. I'll pack my stuff and give you your house back. And your life back."

She caught her breath. "Do you think that's best?"

He nodded. "I owe you an apology, Claire, and I can't blame my mistakes on poor memory. My motivation was purely selfish. I've enjoyed the board's approval. And to be brutally honest, the headmaster's house tempted me greatly." He shook his head, disgusted with himself. "I'm sorry, Claire. You deserve better. I'll be out in half an hour."

Trevor took another long, hungry look at his pretend wife. If he didn't leave now, he'd never leave. He'd live with Claire Jennings, in this tiny cluttered house, forever.

Chapter Eleven

Claire walked around her empty house in utter shock. The evening had turned out much differently than she'd anticipated. Trevor had started to confess and she'd stopped him. But since they hadn't told Granddad the truth, she hadn't expected Trevor would move out. Certainly not tonight.

It's the only way, she reminded herself. But a deep sense of emptiness washed over her. She sank onto the couch, in the same spot where Trevor had kissed her minutes ago, and felt lonelier than she'd felt in her entire life.

At midnight, Claire dragged herself to bed, then lay awake as her digital clock methodically turned over the minutes. Around 4:00 A.M., she drifted into a restless slumber.

The next morning, she got up in a fog and took a long,

hot bath which brought little relief. Midmorning the phone rang. Claire snatched it up and her heart nearly stopped beating when she heard Trevor's voice. "Good morning, Claire."

"Hi, Trevor."

"I did a lot of thinking last night. I've taken unfair advantage of you and I'm deeply sorry. I scheduled a visit with your grandfather on Monday evening and I'll tell him everything. It's the only honorable thing to do."

"I'll go with you. We're both at fault. There's no reason for you to take all the blame."

"Whatever you want."

They ended the conversation quickly and when Claire hung up, she felt even more depressed.

The weekend dragged on forever. She was grateful when Monday morning finally dawned and she could hurry off to school.

The last of the girls scurried into their seats just as the bell rang. Claire took roll, realizing how much things had improved since that first frightening morning in this classroom. That day she'd faced a sea of girls in red jumpers and crisp white blouses and felt panicky about what lay ahead. But each day unfolded a little more smoothly, bonding Claire and her students in significant ways. Her affection for her cherubs, even the ones with tilted haloes, was definitely growing.

Later, the recess bell rang and Claire watched her girls file out of the classroom. As soon as they'd gone, her thoughts again centered on Trevor.

The man had such presence. He filled a room, sucking out most of the available oxygen and leaving her breathless. She missed him terribly. It was like half of herself had suddenly disappeared.

Yesterday she'd bought a box of chocolate doughnuts, wishing with all her heart that she could share the high-cholesterol snack with Trevor. That evening, she took the doughnuts into her spare bedroom and sat cross-legged on the bed that he used to sleep in. She ate five doughnuts all by herself.

The spare bedroom seemed lifeless without him. She checked the closet, hoping he'd left one article of clothing behind. Of course, he hadn't. Not Trevor. She inhaled deeply, hoping to catch a whiff of his delectable cologne but that, too, had evaporated. Every trace of her pretend husband had been brutally excised from the room.

Claire pulled her thoughts back to the present. Recess was nearly over and she needed to escort her students back into the building. As she went out to the playground, she heard shouting. Two fifth-graders argued at the top of their lungs and while Claire wasn't close enough to catch their words, their body language was abundantly clear. Fury sparked from the girls' eyes.

Kelly and Lee Ann appeared on the scene and Claire's heart caught in her throat. She watched as Kelly began talking to one of the girls and Lee Ann to the other.

It didn't help. The younger girls shouted even louder and one of them gave Kelly a shove that nearly knocked her off her feet.

Claire held her breath, half expecting Kelly to fight back. But she didn't. She just kept talking.

Claire spotted Trevor near the scene. It was the first

time she'd seen him since he moved out and just looking at him stirred a longing inside her. He also watched the confrontation. This was Kelly and Lee Ann's big moment and Claire prayed they wouldn't blow it.

The girls kept mediating and the two fifth-graders became somewhat less agitated. Finally, the shouting died down considerably, then stopped altogether. When all four girls walked peaceably toward the building to get in line, Claire wanted to jump for joy! Kelly and Lee Ann had passed their first test as conflict mediators with flying colors!

Trevor caught Claire's eye and her heart started racing. *Does he miss me as much as I miss him?* she wondered.

Thank goodness he'd observed the confrontation first hand. He might not have believed her if she told him what just happened.

Trevor strode toward her looking as incredibly handsome as ever. She detected his marvelous scent before he reached her side. Her joy about the success of her conflict mediators made her want to throw her arms around Trevor's neck and share this glorious moment with him. But she resisted the temptation.

He cleared his throat. "I was surprise at how well Kelly and Lee Ann handled that confrontation. Seems you were right in your selection of conflict mediators."

Claire felt a surge of joy at Trevor's approval. "Thank you. I was very proud of my girls."

All the students had lined up by the door and Claire and Trevor stood alone on the playground. "I've given a lot of thought to your future as a Brookshire teacher,"

Trevor said. "Would you stop by my office after school so we can discuss it?"

"Certainly." A colony of butterflies suddenly dive bombed Claire's stomach. Her eyes caught his and she wondered what he would tell her this afternoon.

He nodded. "I won't detain you. Your students are waiting."

As Claire and her students reentered the building, she realized that one successful incident with Kelly and Lee Ann didn't make her a good teacher. She and Trevor had very different teaching philosophies and he hadn't approved of hers from the beginning. Did he plan to give her notice this afternoon? That thought left her devastated.

She sighed, feeling she'd failed miserably. She wasn't any of the things Granddad fervently wanted her to be. She wasn't a successful teacher. She'd only lasted a few weeks. And she was just as single as ever.

But disappointing Granddad wasn't nearly as devastating as disappointing herself. The goals she'd set, partly to please him, were now her goals. Her dreams, not Granddad's.

As her students settled into their seats, Claire realized she might not be teaching this class much longer. She blinked back tears that sprang unbidden into her eyes. Saying good-bye to her girls would be extremely painful.

Only one thing could be harder than that. Saying good-bye to Trevor.

Claire's stomach churned anxiously as she knocked on Trevor's office door. She had to get this over with. She couldn't live with the suspense a moment longer.

He opened the door. "Come in, Claire."

She went to sit in the chair across from his desk, squaring her shoulders against the pain he would inflict.

"As I said earlier, I want to discuss your teaching career. How do you feel things are going?"

Claire shifted nervously in the chair and had difficulty meeting his gaze. "Pretty well. The girls are much more respectful. And more cooperative, too. And I see a lot of creativity in my students." Claire stopped, realizing that wouldn't impress him. Creativity wasn't Trevor's strong suit.

"Anything else?"

"Only that I feel I'm making progress. I love teaching and I love my girls."

Claire suddenly couldn't endure the pretense a moment longer. "But it doesn't matter what I think, does it? If you're planning to fire me, Trevor, get it over with. I can't hold up to the pressure of your disapproval."

His dark eyes registered surprise and he ran a hand through his hair, resurrecting the cowlick she'd been missing. "I'm sorry if I gave you the wrong impression, Claire. I feel you've come a long way these past few weeks. Your classroom is more orderly and quiet than it was in the beginning. And your insights into the girls' personalities seems right on target."

Claire glanced at him to see if he was teasing but he looked dead serious.

"I was pleased and surprised at how well Kelly and Lee Ann handled the incident on the playground. I have no intention of letting you go, Claire. Quite the contrary. I want you to sign a permanent contract."

Claire's heart began pounding furiously. "You what?"

"I want you to sign a permanent contract," he repeated.

A deep sense of relief washed over her. "I can't believe it. I thought you were giving me notice."

"I'm sorry, Claire. I know our teaching methods differ but the end result is what counts. You'll do great things with this sixth-grade class. You already are."

Trevor looked so pleased with her and so confident about her teaching ability that Claire again wanted to throw her arms around his neck and share the wonder of this moment. But she couldn't. Fortunately, Trevor was still her employer. *That's all he is,* she reminded herself sternly.

But during the two weeks Trevor had lived with her, he'd become more. Much more. He'd become the fascinating, intelligent, dashing "husband" who put her hormones on overload and turned her into a giddy schoolgirl. He'd become the spark of excitement that made each day worthwhile. And he'd also become the man who had stolen her heart.

He took out the contract. "Please sign on the bottom line."

As she walked to his desk and bent to sign the contract, Claire's heart raced frantically as it always did when Trevor was near. When she leaned down, his tantalizing scent again flooded her senses. This time, she didn't hold her breath. She might never be this close to Trevor again and she intended to enjoy every heady second.

She carefully signed CLAIRE ELIZABETH JENNINGS on

the dotted line and for one crazy moment wished she was signing MRS. TREVOR MATHISON.

"There." She handed him the pen. "Thanks for your confidence, Trevor. I won't disappoint you."

"I know that, Claire. You're a darned good teacher."

Her eyes filled with tears. Trevor's approval flooded her with joy, meaning even more than the approval she had so desperately sought from her grandfather.

Granddad. That nightmare still lay ahead.

"Shall I pick you up tonight? A little before seven?" he asked.

"That would be fine."

Trevor nodded. "See you then."

Claire left the headmaster's office with two emotions warring inside of her. The sheer joy she felt at succeeding as a Brookshire teacher kept bumping up against the deep sense of separation she felt from Trevor. And if that wasn't enough, she had to face the frightful task of telling Granddad that her marriage to Trevor was only make-believe.

As Trevor backed the Jag out of the garage and headed for Mulberry Lane, he pondered the dreadful state his life was in. He'd made a king-sized fool of himself and after tonight that would no longer be a well-kept secret between himself and Claire. Once Jacob Lawrence knew the truth, and shared that information with the Board of Directors, Trevor's happy life as Headmaster of Brookshire School for Young Ladies would be history. But he couldn't live this duplicitous life any longer. So whatever the consequences, he would face them like a man.

Trevor hoped Claire's job wouldn't be affected by the upheaval that was coming. She was turning into an excellent teacher and he wanted her to stay on at Brookshire. How ironic. Just two weeks ago, he'd fought against hiring Claire and now he sincerely wanted her to stay.

In the few days they'd been apart, he missed her more than he'd dreamed possible. When he came home to his neat apartment after school each evening, it seemed sterile and lifeless. His orderly living quarters no longer held the appeal they had before he moved to Mulberry Lane.

He'd tossed throw pillows on the living room floor and even piled some textbooks around them. But the scene was incomplete. He needed Claire sitting in the middle of the mess to make it real.

And to his great surprise, his life had become boring and predictable since he'd moved back home. Nobody meditated and nobody set fires. While living with Claire, he'd grown accustomed to the unexpected which happened on a daily basis and he missed it terribly.

After parking the Jag in her driveway, Trevor went to knock on the door. Claire answered and he spotted stage two blotches on her neck. But even in her obviously stressed state, she looked incredible.

Black stretch pants and a turquoise sweater defined the figure that had so often set fire to his emotions and sent his heart rate soaring. Her shimmery blond hair danced around her shoulders and Trevor wanted to reach out and touch it. He remembered how incredibly silky it felt.

Claire's fascinating blue eyes studied him intently. "Hello, Trevor."

"How are you, Claire?"

"Worried and a little scared. After tonight, my relationship with Granddad will end."

Seeing her sadness, Trevor wanted to pull her into his arms and kiss away her pain. But he couldn't. He had caused the pain.

"Your grandfather won't blame you, Claire. I'm the bad guy. He'll ask me to resign."

"Oh, surely not. You're a wonderful headmaster. Granddad won't ask you to leave Brookshire."

He shrugged. "I wish I shared your confidence. Well, let's go. We can't put this off any longer."

He walked her to the Jag and helped her in. "Tonight's visit will be a lot different from our last one. Your grandfather won't be offering us a house or a honeymoon."

Claire sighed. "We're missing out on a lot, aren't we, Trevor?"

"Sure seems that way."

He realized there'd be much more important things he'd miss out on. Tonight would end his relationship with Claire—both personally and professionally. He couldn't even imagine that. Life without her seemed unbelievably bleak.

She fell silent, leaving him alone with his apprehensions. Over the last few days, a disconcerting question had nagged at him. Was he falling in love with Claire? He kept pushing the thought aside, but it always resurfaced.

His past history made him leery of falling in love. He'd loved Jessica with all his heart and she'd betrayed him. The memory of that relationship was actually helping him now. It kept him in line, helped him stay in control. It stopped him from reaching over right this minute, taking Claire's hand, and begging her to become his wife.

Good thing. If he touched her, he'd lose the tenuous grip he still had on his emotions. Control was the only thing he had left. He'd long since sold his dignity and self-respect down the river. If he wanted to salvage what he still could of his rapidly disintegrating life, he must stay in control.

Trevor pulled into Jacob Lawrence's driveway and he and Claire walked solemnly down the cobblestone walk to the front door. A cool breeze ruffled the silky curls around her face and it was all Trevor could do not to reach out and caress them. He knew from experience that her hair felt soft as silk. The thought of never touching Claire again haunted him. With a heavy heart, he rang the bell.

Chairman Lawrence opened the door. "Welcome, kids. Come on in." He ushered them to the library where they took the same seats they'd occupied when he'd shown them the architect's drawings. "Now what's this important information you want to share? Don't tell me you're postponing the honeymoon?"

Trevor cleared his throat. "I'd like to speak first, sir, if I may."

Chairman Lawrence nodded and Trevor scraped together his faltering courage. "Remember the morning you stopped by Claire's house, saw the auto club receipt on the coffee table, and assumed that Claire and I were married?"

"Of course, I remember. Why do you ask?"

"Well, I should have corrected you immediately, sir. Because that was a false assumption."

A scowl darkened the Chairman's face. "What do you mean, a false assumption? I saw 'Mrs. Trevor Mathison' on that receipt. In Claire's handwriting."

Claire couldn't just sit by and watch while her life fell apart. "Let me start from the beginning, Granddad," she said, hoping that for once he'd listen. Really listen.

"You see, Granddad, when Trevor interviewed me for the Brookshire position, I accidentally left my briefcase in his office. He returned it later that afternoon, and because he seemed incredibly stressed, I gave him some herb tea and massaged his shoulders. Trevor relaxed a lot," she said, "and then he fell asleep in my recliner. I didn't have the heart to wake him so . . ."

Granddad's dark gaze penetrated hers, going straight for her heart. "I don't need all the specifics, Claire, just the bottom line. Are you confirming what Trevor just said? That you and he aren't really married?"

Claire's heart felt like a broken elevator racing down an empty shaft. "That's right, Granddad."

Her grandfather stood and started pacing, obviously trying to assimilate the shocking information. Claire sat very still as she anticipated Granddad's wrath, immediately forthcoming.

When he finally spoke, it wasn't with the booming voice she'd anticipated. He was surprisingly controlled. "So all of this was one big hoax, huh? You pulled the wool over my eyes." He looked more hurt than angry.

Claire would have preferred that he shout his disapproval to the rooftops rather than voice it so quietly.

"I'm truly sorry, Granddad," she said, meaning it with her whole heart. "All I ever wanted to do was please you." She shook her head. "I never seem able to live up to your expectations."

"That's ridiculous, Claire. You're living up to my expectations right now. You're doing extremely well as a Brookshire teacher. Isn't that right, Trevor?"

"She certainly is," Trevor confirmed, and Claire felt grateful that her career was on track. Would that be enough to appease her grandfather? Or herself?

Granddad shook his head. "I can't believe you two aren't married." His eyes suddenly narrowed. "Let me ask you one question. Do you love each other?"

The library grew as silent as a deserted playground. Claire looked at Trevor and saw the torture she felt mirrored in his dark eyes. In that painful moment, she realized, without a doubt, that she loved Trevor Mathison. Loved him desperately, hopelessly, completely.

But that didn't matter, because he didn't love her. She drove him crazy. He'd made that abundantly clear.

Trevor came to her rescue and for once she was grateful. "We've only known each other two weeks, sir. That isn't long enough to fall in love."

"I beg to differ," Granddad said tersely. "Sara and I fell in love that quickly and shared a wonderful life together. But that's beside the point. I'd never encourage people to marry unless they are deeply in love."

Granddad shook his head. "You kids had me buffaloed. I thought you had the real thing . . . the once-in-a-lifetime love that the whole world is searching for. I must say I'm disappointed. Much more for the two of you than for myself."

"Things should have never gotten out of hand the way they did," Claire said softly.

Now Trevor stood and started pacing. "We couldn't live this deceitful life any longer, sir. I've moved back to my apartment and Claire and I are anxious to set the record straight." He stopped and looked at Granddad. "I want you to know that I accept full responsibility for everything that's happened. If you wish, I'll resign immediately. But I hope you won't let any of this affect Claire's position at Brookshire."

Granddad glared at Trevor. "Just sit down and be quiet, son. Give a man a chance to think."

Trevor sank onto the couch beside Claire and Granddad took over the pacing. It was like passing the baton in the Olympics.

He went the full length of the library, then turned and came back the other direction. He stopped, stroked his chin, and stared off into space.

As the tension built, Claire realized that she could soon lose these two men who meant the world to her. Their faults suddenly dimmed as she considered life without them. She couldn't imagine how grim and lonely it would be.

Impulsively, she reached for Trevor's hand, needing to touch him while she still could. When he squeezed her hand in return, a thrill coursed through her and her pulse raced. But her heart felt like it would surely break.

Granddad finally settled in his leather high-backed

armchair and crossed his legs. Claire held her breath, waiting for him to issue another ultimatum.

"I see all of this differently than you do," he finally said. "I don't feel that you were living a double life. Neither one of you has a deceitful bone in your body."

Claire couldn't believe her ears. "How can you say that? Trevor and I pretended . . ."

"Maybe there wasn't as much pretending going on as you thought. From the first time I saw you together, I believed that you loved each other. But you're obviously not smart enough to figure that out for yourselves." He shook his head. "I'm disappointed, but not because you deceived me. I'm disappointed that you don't see what a wonderful relationship you have. What a great life you could share."

Claire and Trevor exchanged surprised glances.

Granddad leaned forward. "Everyone else sees it: The board members, their wives, the teachers at Brookshire. And I'm certain that your students figured it out long ago." He shook his head. "It's the two of you who don't get it. You're so busy trying to do the right thing in everyone else's eyes that you're missing out on the greatest thing in the world. The deep love between a man and a woman."

Claire glanced at Trevor, surprised to see his agonized expression. For once he was letting his emotions show.

Granddad stood. "You kids will have to work out your own problems and I'll respect whatever decision you make about your future. But there's no need to consider resigning. I want you both to stay on at Brookshire."

Claire felt a flood of relief, much more for Trevor than

herself. At least the man she loved wouldn't be hurt anymore than he'd already been hurt.

"I'm going to the club for a while. Don't you two leave here until you've had a long, honest talk about your feelings for each other. That's an order." He left the room, closing the door behind him.

Claire's hands broke out in a cold sweat as the room suddenly became as silent as a tomb. The only sound was grandfather—the clock, this time, not the man.

Trevor resumed pacing. Then stopped abruptly and faced her. "What do you think of your grandfather's remarks?"

Claire got to her feet. "I, I don't know what to think," she stammered. She couldn't tell Trevor that she thought Granddad was absolutely right. That all she wanted was to spend the rest of her life with him. That she didn't care if he paced. Didn't care if he alphabetized their breakfast cereals and spices. Didn't care if he organized the heck out of their home, wherever it was. She'd live with him in her cluttered little house, or in his antiseptically clean apartment, or in the headmaster's house on the Brookshire campus. Any place would be home if Trevor were there.

But she couldn't tell him her feelings. She wouldn't lay her heart out before him like an area rug and have him pace all over it!

Trevor came to her, cupped her chin in his hand and gazed into her eyes. "There's been more than enough pretending in this relationship. I want an honest answer, Claire. Do you love me?"

She couldn't help herself. She blurted out the truth.

"Yes, Trevor. I love you. I think I've loved you from the first moment I saw you. I love you with all my heart." She squared her shoulders, waiting for him to say that he didn't share her feelings.

To her surprise, he pulled her into his arms, and buried his face in her neck. "Oh, Claire. My own, precious, darling Claire. I love you more than life itself."

Relief washed over her. Relief, and joy, and wonder, and excitement. She smoothed back Trevor's cowlick and kissed his forehead. "Do you mean what you just said, Trevor Mathison, or are you lying again? You've gotten pretty proficient at it these past few weeks."

He chuckled and his warm breath on her neck sent shivers of delight racing through her body. "I mean every word. You and I will never lie about anything again. We'll be the most honest, predictable married couple on Mulberry Lane. Why poor Mrs. Darling will be downright bored by our proper, middle-class behavior."

Claire lifted an eyebrow. "Was there a proposal in there somewhere? Did I miss it?"

When he looked deeply into her eyes, his runaway charisma left her weak and light headed. "Claire, my darling. Will you marry me?"

"Oh, yes, Trevor. Yes, yes, yes!"

When Trevor kissed her, the sensation of his lips claiming hers set off fireworks inside Claire that rivaled any ballpark display. After the most exhilarating kiss of her life, she snuggled as close to Trevor as she could get, marveling in his strength, his masculinity, but mostly in wonder of his love.

He broke away first. "Let's get going, babe. We've got a big night ahead."

Claire had difficulty pulling herself out of the magic of Trevor's embrace. She felt dreamy—one step removed from reality. She could probably give up meditation because kissing Trevor produced the same results in a much more exhilarating fashion.

"What do you mean a big night? I thought we'd just go to my place and . . ."

"Oh, no. We're going to do this right. First, I'm taking you to dinner to celebrate our engagement. And after that, we'll find a justice of the peace who's open all night."

Claire giggled. "I don't believe it, Trevor. You're being impulsive!"

He grinned. "You should have warned me that it's contagious."

As Claire bent to pick up her purse, a powerful realization flooded her. "Trevor! We can actually use all those wedding gifts that you filed alphabetically in my basement! We won't have to return a single one!"

He looked smug. "I knew my work would pay off."

They left Granddad's and walked out to the Jag. The velvety sky was studded with stars and the moon slipped behind a cloud, illuminating it with a lining of delicate silver. The wonder of the night reaffirmed the wonder of the love Claire felt for Trevor.

The temperature had dropped and when she shivered Trevor pulled her close. "When we get home, I know which present we'll use first."

Claire looked at him curiously. "Which one?"

"The dual-control, radiation-protected blanket from our neighbors."

"We won't be needing that blanket, sweetheart." She linked her arms around Trevor's neck and kissed him as intensely and thoroughly as she knew how.

When the kiss ended, Trevor stepped back and took a stabilizing breath. "You just won that argument, Mrs. Mathison. We'll exchange the blanket after school tomorrow."